2-

TAKEN

Michael J. Totten

Michael J. Totten is a foreign correspondent and foreign policy analyst who has reported from the Middle East, the Balkans, and the former Soviet Union.

He's a contributing editor at *World Affairs* and *City Journal*. His work has also appeared in the *New York Times,* the *Wall Street Journal, The New Republic, Slake: Los Angeles, Reason, Commentary,* the *New York Daily News, LA Weekly,* the *Jerusalem Post,* and Beirut's *Daily Star.*

His first book, *The Road to Fatima Gate,* won the Washington Institute Silver Book Prize in 2011. He won the 2007 Weblog Award for Best Middle East or Africa Blog, he won it again in 2008, and he was named Blogger of the Year in 2006 by *The Week* magazine for his dispatches from the Middle East. He lives with his wife in Oregon and is a former resident of Beirut.

Visit his blog at www.MichaelTotten.com.

ALSO BY MICHAEL J. TOTTEN

The Road to Fatima Gate
In the Wake of the Surge
Where the West Ends

TAKEN

MICHAEL J. TOTTEN

First American edition published in 2013 by Belmont Estate Books

Cover design by Kathleen Lynch
Edited by Elissa Englund

Manufactured in the United States on acid-free paper

FIRST AMERICAN EDITION

Totten, Michael J.
Taken: A Novel
ISBN-13: 9780615750965
ISBN-10: 0615750966

For my brother

Contents

"It is normal to give away a little of one's life in order not to lose it all." —Albert Camus

"I had been, you know, held in the closet for two months and ... abused in all manner of ways. I was very good at doing what I was told." —Patty Hearst

PART ONE

SMASHED AND GRABBED

Chapter One

They took me from my house in the night. Rough hands slapped duct tape over my mouth and I sat up in bed, head swirling with gray shapes and vertigo, wondering if I was dreaming, but before I could yell, before I could reach up and rip off the tape, two hundred pounds of muscle and purpose shoved me back down onto the bed.

My wife was out of town teaching a class in Seattle, and I hadn't bothered to turn on the alarm system or the motion detector downstairs. I didn't hear the back door open, nor did our cats alert me that dangerous strangers had entered our home. I kicked with both legs but only flailed against my own sheets and blankets. A mass of hands gripped me, flipped me onto my stomach, and jammed my face into the pillow. I could hardly breathe as steel cuffs slammed around my wrists, the metal digging hard against bone.

For a moment I thought I was being arrested, that police officers had raided the wrong house, that I'd be released soon enough—and with an apology—after they took me down to the station and realized they had the wrong guy.

The moment was fleeting. I will never forget the sound of the voice I heard next: calm, professional, and chillingly void of emotion.

"Get the blindfold on him."

The man who uttered those words, I knew, would gut me as remorselessly as he would crush a beetle under his boot.

Get the blindfold on him.

Quick and certain, with just the slightest touch of impatience.

Get the blindfold on him.

Unaccented American English from a man who couldn't be over

thirty.

Get the blindfold on him.

They tied what felt like a pillowcase over my eyes. It covered everything from my nose to my forehead. No chance I could sneak a peek over the top or under the bottom. Two hands gripped each of my thrashing limbs and hauled me off the bed and down the stairs. I heard what sounded like work boots on hardwood, but their hands on my skin felt soft, not like those of laborers. I managed to fling an arm free and knock a picture frame off the wall, but they restrained me again and dragged me out the back and into the driveway at the side of the house.

A van door slid open. As I struggled to yell through the duct tape, they dumped me onto the van's grooved metal floor. Two men climbed in with me, each holding one of my arms. The other two hopped in front. When I heard the ignition turn over, I arched my back and kicked one of the bastards. Either a fist or an elbow—I couldn't be sure—slammed into my mouth, mashing lips against teeth.

I tasted blood and iron and smelled body odor—theirs—as we hurtled down surface streets, the van's engine gunning like a getaway car, and merged onto the interstate.

My name is Michael Totten, and I work as a foreign correspondent in the Middle East. For ten years I feared something like this might happen. It's a hazard of my profession.

Khaled Sheikh Mohamed kidnapped my colleague Daniel Pearl in Pakistan and beheaded him on camera with a kitchen knife. Murderous drug cartels south of the border have turned Mexico into one of the most dangerous countries on earth to work as a reporter. During the Lebanese civil war in the 1980s, Hezbollah kidnapped journalists and chained them to radiators. I'm always taking a risk when I leave the comforts of home to report from the unfortunate parts of the world. I was especially concerned about being snatched off the street during my seven trips to Iraq, but I had no idea I'd ever be yanked out of bed in my hometown in Oregon.

Nobody said anything as we drove. Whoever these guys were, they weren't talking. I tried to curse them but could only groan into the tape over my mouth. All I could hear was the thrum of the engine and the vibration of the wheels at interstate speed. If I'd been congested and couldn't breathe through my nose, I would have suffocated.

The van's floor dug into my back. My wrists ached from the handcuffs, and a muscle in my right shoulder cramped up. I noticed the smell of sweat in the blindfold that covered most of my face and realized it was my own.

After hours had passed, we finally stopped. It felt like four hours, but it must have only been three. Surely my sense of time was distorted. At least I no longer cringed and expected to be punched or elbowed again.

The man in the passenger seat got out and unscrewed the van's gas cap. I listened carefully. Was anyone else out there? Would a gas-station attendant see or hear me if I kicked and thrashed and made a big enough scene? Did the van even have windows? I imagined it probably didn't.

But there was no attendant. Nobody asked how much gas or what kind we wanted. I heard the man from the passenger seat swipe a credit card and insert the nozzle into the tank.

We were no longer in Oregon then. Self-service at gas stations is illegal in Oregon. You have to wait for an attendant to fill the tank for you. So at some point in the night, we had crossed into Washington. It had to be Washington. My house in Portland is just a fifteen-minute drive to the state line, but California and Idaho are six hours away. Nevada is eight hours away. Canada is also six hours away, and there was no chance I'd missed an international border crossing.

We left the station and after another hour or so, the van slowed and turned. The tires crunched onto gravel. I braced myself. This was it. Wherever we were going, we had arrived.

The man in the passenger seat climbed out and opened the sliding side door. The scent of pine overwhelmed me at once. We were in a forest, or very near one, and we were on the dry eastern side of the

Cascade Mountains rather than the wet western side, where the forests are fir. I figured we must be somewhere in the vicinity of Yakima or possibly Ellensburg, a college town in the middle of the state.

The duct tape over my mouth was ripped away stingingly.

"Will you walk?" It was that voice again. The one that said "Get the blindfold on him."

"I'll walk," I said, "if you take off the blindfold."

"Get him in the house," he said, and I felt myself being hoisted by my shoulders, the tops of my bare toes trailing in gravel. "Go ahead and scream if you want. No one will hear you out here."

A supernova of hatred exploded inside me. If they looked like they were going to kill me, I'd fight them. And if they kept me in cuffs and held down my legs, I'd bite the bastards' fingers off with my teeth.

They took me inside, dragged me into a basement, and sat my ass down in a straight-backed wooden chair no softer than the van floor. They uncuffed one of my wrists and recuffed it to a table leg. I heard heavy booted footsteps heading up wooden stairs toward the main part of the house.

I sat hunched over in absolute silence with my shoulders nearly up to my ears. I figured they'd left me alone, but when I reached up with my one free hand to take off my blindfold, I saw sitting before me a man of about thirty with blue eyes, dark curls, and light brown skin. With a face like that, he could have been from a number of places around the world. Italy, Chile, and Armenia come to mind now, but I knew at the time he was almost certainly an Arab. He could have been from Pakistan or Iran, but I doubted it.

Behind him stood a hairy bear of a man with black eyes, a long black beard, and short-cropped hair. He was the one who had punched me. I could tell. He had an *I like to kick the shit out of people* look on his face.

"Michael," the blue-eyed man said. "Believe me, it is a pleasure to finally meet you."

I stared at him and tried as hard as I could to show no expression. No anger. No fear. Then I sucked my teeth hard enough to make my split lip bleed again, leaned to the side, and spit blood onto the floor.

"Sorry about that," the man said. "But you were flailing about and kicked Mahmoud here in the ribs."

The larger man stood with his arms folded and drummed his fingers on his biceps at the sound of his name. I turned and wiped the blood off my lips and onto my shoulder.

"My name is Ahmed," the blue-eyed man said.

"Ahmed what?" I said. "What's your last name?" I've spent enough time in the Arab world that I can sometimes tell which country people are from by their last names.

"Just Ahmed for now," he said. "We have a job for you."

"I'm not working for you," I said. "Shoot me if you want, but I'm not going to help you."

I honestly didn't know if I meant that or not. They expected me to resist and they weren't beating me up, so what was I supposed to say? Sure, okay, I'll do what you want?

"I can understand your reluctance," Ahmed said, "but you will do what we say."

I looked at him and said nothing.

"We aren't necessarily going to kill you or even hurt you," he said. "As long as you do what we say. If you cooperate, we'll see what happens."

He could tell by the look on my face that I didn't buy it.

He sighed. "If I told you we'd let you go if you cooperate, would you believe me?"

"No," I said.

"Okay then," he said. "I didn't think so. So I won't insult your intelligence."

"What do you want with me, Ahmed?" I started grinding my teeth. I resisted clenching my hands into fists, but I couldn't help grinding my teeth.

"I appreciate that you're pronouncing my name correctly," he said.

The *h* in his name is aspirated. It's pronounced like the *h* in *house*.

"Of course I know how to say *Ahmed*," I said. "I've been working in and writing about the Arab world for ten years."

"Yes," he said and smiled. "I know. That's why we picked you."

"Why me?" I said.

"I just told you," he said.

"No, I mean why me of all the American journalists who cover the Middle East? Why not kidnap Peter Bergen or Tom Friedman? They're both more famous than I am."

"Because," he said and stood up. "You have a widely read blog. And you're going to give us the password."

I had a blog at the Web site of *The Global Weekly*, where I published a weekly column, daily takes on the news of the world, and occasional long dispatches from war zones and trouble spots. I could write whatever I wanted. Unlike traditional journalism, my work was published instantly and unedited with the click of a mouse. If Ahmed had my password, he could hijack my column and publish whatever he wanted himself.

Mahmoud unfolded a four-inch Leatherman knife and flicked his thumb across the blade sideways. It took everything I had, but I resisted.

"I'm not giving you the password," I said and swallowed hard. My hands felt clammy, and it was all I could do to keep myself from shaking.

"Cut off his eyelids," Ahmed said.

Mahmoud grunted and stepped forward, the cords standing out in his neck. I spasmed as though I had just been zapped with a cattle prod.

"Okayokayokay," I said and gave up the password.

"That wasn't so difficult, was it?" Ahmed said. "You will do what we say. And it will be easier on everyone here if you immediately do what we say. Don't ever say no to me again."

I tried hard not to breathe too heavily, but it was difficult.

"You kidnapped me just to get my blog's password?" I said.

"That's just for backup," he said. "For insurance, you might say."

"Against what?" I said.

"Insubordination," he said. "If you don't do what we say, Mahmoud will cut off your eyelids, take a nice pretty picture, and upload the photograph to your blog. Even your wife and mother will get a good hard look at what's happening to you."

Chapter Two

They left me to sleep cuffed to the table, but the table wasn't bolted to the floor. To free myself, all I had to do was lift it up and slide my wrist off.

There wasn't much else in the room. Just the table, the two chairs, and two bare 40-watt lightbulbs hanging from exposed wires. Aside from a door leading to a half bathroom (at least I had a sink to wash in, if not a shower) and thirteen steps leading to a closed and, no doubt, bolted wooden door into the house—which in my mind's eye led to the kitchen—the room they held me in was an empty containment space. They left me with no tools, no books, no television, no refrigerator, nothing soft to sit on, no means of escape, nothing at all.

At least there were four little windows so I could see out. I was able to open three of them, but they were too small to slip through. Though it was late summer, the dry season in the Pacific Northwest, rain had fallen recently. Water had pooled underneath the windows after leaking or flooding in. Most of it had already dried, but it left watermarks on the poured-concrete floor.

Outside, a grassy field stretched a hundred or so feet from the house—it was hard to judge distances in the dark, but the moon was out and I could sort of see—until it reached the edge of the pine forest. I deeply inhaled the rich and slightly spicy smell of the trees and listened carefully. I heard crickets, a gentle wind in the boughs, and a distant jet heading to or from Seattle, but I couldn't hear any traffic or movement. No one would hear me if I yelled—I was sure of it. Ahmed and the others wouldn't have put me there if anyone else had a house within a mile.

They were smart to bring me to the eastern side of the state. Most of it's empty.

The western slopes of the Cascades, a chain of active stratovolcanoes two miles high located just fifty miles east of Seattle and Portland, are wet places. The crest of the range is so high that storms off the Pacific Ocean slam into the mountains, where the peaks and the crags wring nearly every last drop of moisture out of the clouds. This creates dry conditions and even deserts on the eastern side, a rain shadow where water is scarce and the land is much harder. Few choose to scratch out a living there. The overwhelming majority of Pacific Northwesterners live in Oregon's lush Willamette Valley and along Washington's Puget Sound, a vast island-studded coastal inlet bounded on the east and the west by glaciated peaks.

I learned how to survive in both our wet and dry wilderness areas when I was eight years old. It was part of our grade-school curriculum. I know how to find water. I know how to find and trap food. I know how to build a shelter without any tools. If I could escape from that basement and get a running head start into the wild, Ahmed and his crew would never find me. I even fantasized about hunting them down and picking them off one by one if they came after me. It wouldn't be hard. I'd need tools for that, but not many.

But I was trapped. The ceiling was suffocatingly low. I could not stand up straight without hitting my head on the exposed wooden sub-flooring above. The boards smelled faintly of heating oil and mold. The house had been there a long time. I idly wondered what style it was. There was no telling from the basement. And since I was blindfolded when they brought me in, all I could do was guess.

Leaning on one of the windows, I saw a faint glow in the sky just above the tree line. It was dawn getting ready to break. So I knew now which way was east. East was the wall to the right of the stairs. I'd been up most of the night and should have been exhausted, but my hands wouldn't stop shaking. My veins ran hot and I felt an urgent clawing sensation in my chest.

There's only so much adrenaline in the human body. Eventually I'd have to calm down, but I couldn't yet, not when I still didn't know what they wanted from me and had no idea if and when I would ever get out of there.

I lay down on the wooden table. It was softer than the floor, but who was I kidding? I couldn't sleep. I just lay there and thought about my wife and cats, wondering how long it would take them to figure out that I was not coming back.

I ached for my wife. I would have given anything at that moment to spoon with her in bed, to breathe softly on the back of her neck while curled up safely behind our locked doors.

If I couldn't escape, those men were going to kill me. I'd already seen two of their faces. I could describe them to a sketch artist and identify them in a lineup. At some point the one they called Mahmoud would walk through the door and come down the stairs and slit my throat with that Leatherman knife. No matter what I did, no matter what I said, no matter how much I cooperated and prostrated myself, they were going to kill me.

I slid off the table and onto the floor. At some point I fell asleep and half woke again and in my delirious state forgot where I was. What was I doing on the floor? Did I fall off the bed in the night? Why didn't Shelly shake me awake and say, "Sweetie, come back in the bed"? Then I remembered. It was the rudest awakening I'd ever had. I covered my eyes with the crook of my elbow, ground my teeth hard, and imagined tearing four men apart with my hands.

Ahmed jolted me awake in the morning. "Michael!" he said as he descended the stairs. It took me a moment to fully wake up and remember that he was dangerous.

"You got your wrist off the table leg," he said.

"Wasn't difficult," I said. I sat up and winced. The concrete floor was killing my back. I rubbed my face and realized that the pair of handcuffs still dangled from my right wrist. My left wrist was free, but I needed a key to get the damn things all the way off.

"Listen," he said. "I'd like for us to start over. Mahmoud is fixing you eggs, toast, and tea. Would you like some juice too? We have apple and orange."

I blinked at him and expected him to sit, if not on the floor then at least in the chair, but he remained standing.

"What do you want from me?" I said.

"We need you to write for us."

"To write for you," I said.

"That's right," he said. "We need you to write about us and what's happening to you on your blog. Mahmoud will bring a laptop down for you, stripped of a network card, of course. We can't have you sending emails to the police. You compose entries for your blog and we'll upload them for you. That's why we needed your password last night. We don't want to mutilate your face and post bloody pictures. That would not speak to our … purpose."

"If you want to hack into my blog and publish terrorist propaganda," I said, "why not just write it yourself? You have the password. You can publish whatever you want. I can't stop you. My editors will pull the plug on it once they've figured out what you've done, but it will be up there for a while."

"We aren't interested in propaganda," he said. "You can write whatever you want."

Was I supposed to believe this?

"What do you mean, I can write whatever I want?"

"Just open the word processor on the laptop, type whatever you want, and we'll upload it to your blog at the magazine. You can call us terrorists if you like. We won't even stop you from lying. Tell the world we've pulled out your fingernails if it makes you feel better. I'm going to ask you to be honest. We haven't pulled out your fingernails. If you lie, you will be violating your journalistic integrity. That's on you. But I don't expect you to be unbiased. You can hate us in print all you like. We just want you to write about us and your time here."

I looked at him sideways.

"Why?" I said. "You want to read about yourself on the Internet?"

"I don't want to read about myself on the Internet. What I want is for other people to read about me on the Internet. You remember the Unabomber?"

"Of course," I said.

"You remember that the *New York Times* and the *Washington Post* published his manifesto?"

"Of course," I said.

"Did you read it?" he said.

I shook my head.

"Neither did I," he said. "I was just a kid at the time, but I don't know anyone who actually read what he wrote. Instead, everyone read about it. Everyone was told he was an environmentalist wacko, but hardly anyone paid attention to what he actually said. I still haven't read what he wrote and I don't plan to, but he was an object lesson for us. I could write a manifesto. Maybe it would be published and maybe it wouldn't. Either way, hardly anyone would actually read it. I'd be dismissed as an extremist—as a terrorist even—and anything I say will be quickly forgotten. But what you write will be read. And it won't be forgotten. No one has ever blogged from captivity. You're a professional. And you're famous. You're all over the news now."

I could see his logic, but I didn't believe for a minute that he would actually let me write whatever I wanted. I did relax a bit, though. If he wanted to use me for propaganda purposes, he would at least let me live for a while.

"Not only will millions of people read whatever you write," he said. "Millions will look at your blog every day to see if you've published anything new."

That would only be true if my editors didn't shut down the blog, but I didn't say that.

"Every time someone looks at your blog," he said, "even if you haven't posted anything fresh, they'll be thinking of me. And they'll be thinking about our political cause."

I wasn't exactly sure what his cause was, but his political orientation was hardly a mystery. His sidekick Mahmoud groomed himself like a Salafist. The Salafists are reactionary Sunni Muslims, the Taliban of the Arab world. Mahmoud's long bushy beard and short cropped hair made him obvious, at least to me.

The door at the top of the stairs opened and Mahmoud pounded down the steps in his work boots. He carried my breakfast on a tray. Scrambled eggs and wheat toast on a plate, a plain white mug with a floating mint tea bag, and a small glass of what appeared to be apple juice. He gently placed it in front of me and went back upstairs.

I resisted the instinctive urge to thank him, the man who split my lip and came at me with a knife the evening before. Ahmed did it for me. "*Shukran*," he said. *Thank you* in Arabic.

"*Afwan*," Mahmoud said. *You're welcome.*

I felt a small twinge of guilt for not saying thank you myself, almost like I was kid again and my embarrassed parents had yet to teach me my manners. I was pretty sure, though, that Ahmed wanted me to feel that way. He was being manipulative.

The pair of handcuffs still dangled from my right wrist. I was tempted to lunge at him, swing my arm in a wide arc, and feel the satisfying crack of torqued steel smashing into his cheekbone. I knew, though, that Mahmoud would make me regret it. They both would.

Cut off his eyelids. That's what Ahmed had calmly told that bucket of hair and muscle and fat the previous night.

"So what's your big cause?" I said.

"It shouldn't be hard for you to figure it out," he said.

"Right," I said. "Don't tell me. You hate America."

"I don't hate America," he said. "I was born in Seattle. You and I are practically neighbors. Portland is, what, a three-hour drive from downtown Seattle? No, if I hated America, I would be hating myself. And I can't very well hate myself, can I?"

I sighed. "What then? You hate the Jewish lobby and the Zionist

Entity."

"What I hate is American policy," he said.

"Everyone has problems with American policy," I said. "That's what protests, elections, and letters to the editor are for. No one else here kidnaps anybody. Just you."

"Ah," he said. "But that isn't true. You know that isn't true. It should be true, but it's not. And that's why you're here. That's why we're holding you."

"What are you talking about?" I said.

"Guantánamo Bay," he said. I swallowed hard. "Your government, our government, is holding 169 hostages in a prison at Guantánamo Bay in Cuba. We want them released. We demand they be released. When they go free, you can go free."

I felt like my insides had just fallen onto the floor. The prisoners at Guantánamo Bay were captured on battlefields in Afghanistan. Ahmed wanted to exchange me for *them*? The United States government doesn't swap prisoners with terrorists. If Ahmed, Mahmoud, and the others weren't messing around, if they really wouldn't let me go until the others were free, I'd never see my wife or anyone else but these four again.

Chapter Three

Everyone has a place where they come from. Mine is the Pacific Northwest of the United States of America.

My home is in Portland, a metropolitan area of more than two million people, but even the city center feels at times like an urban encampment amid a vast wilderness. From downtown on a clear day, I can see the glacier-covered peaks of the high Cascades and the temperate rainforests beneath them. The beach is but a leisurely drive from my house. It's not only the edge of the continent. It's the terminus of Western civilization.

The western United States, settled by adventurous pioneers, is the "America" of America. The east is our "Europe." A spirit of rugged individualism exists out here that has been tempered by age and by time in cities like New York and Boston. Just thirty minutes from downtown Portland remains a wilderness so vast, you can vanish into it forever if you're unlucky or stupid. At night it's as dark as it was when a Lemhi Shoshone woman named Sacagawea led Meriwether Lewis and William Clark out here in the early nineteenth century on a quest underwritten by Thomas Jefferson.

I am a product of this place. I didn't move here from somewhere else like so many of my friends and neighbors. But I've also transcended it. Not until I spent some quality time in the broken parts of the world did I truly learn to appreciate what I have. I don't only mean the natural beauty, the mild climate, the prosperity, and the political freedom that's so easy to take for granted. Even the little things get me when I come home. Pushing a shopping cart down the well-stocked cereal aisle in a Whole Foods or a Safeway is an extraordinary experience after returning from Baghdad.

The Pacific Northwest is devoid of oppression and conflict. There's little recorded history of armed struggle here. Nobody sets off any car bombs. We don't have a police state. Local governments are mostly run by middle-class people. Militias and death squads are unthinkable. War is but a tragic abstraction that inflicts its damages on places most of us never see. Those who spend their entire lives here can easily form a warped view of the world and human nature, albeit a pleasant one.

Should I envy such people? Honestly, I don't know. My work as a war correspondent has darkened my outlook, but I'm not scarred. It has also, at the same time, made me appreciate our region of light more than I ever did growing up.

As far as I know, no American before me had ever been kidnapped inside the United States for a prisoner exchange by Middle Eastern terrorists, but it has happened in Israel. Remember Gilad Shalit? He was the young Israeli soldier kidnapped and held by Hamas in Gaza for more than five years. He was released in 2011 in exchange for more than one thousand Palestinian prisoners, many of them convicted terrorists.

It was a lopsided deal that made no kind of sense whatsoever, but Israeli society went nuts over Gilad Shalit. His name was in the news every day. Activists camped out on the streets of Jerusalem near the prime minister's office and refused to go home until he was freed. The government faced relentless pressure from every sector of the society for years and finally had to relent. Not even the hard-line government of Benjamin Netanyahu could resist that pressure forever. I could only imagine how much more intense the campaign to free Shalit would have been had he been blogging about his captivity in a widely read online magazine. It would have been extraordinary. The prisoner exchange almost certainly would have happened much faster.

That's what Ahmed wanted with me. I could certainly see his logic. My job at *The Global Weekly* was an unusual one. I filed regular dispatches from places like terrorized Lebanon, revolutionary Egypt, and war-torn Iraq. But since I had a blog, I could write whatever I wanted without having to clear story ideas with editors. My work was not even spell-checked by editors. I just wrote whatever I felt like on a given day in Microsoft Word, copied and pasted the text into the blogging software, clicked Publish, and *voilà*. My work instantly appeared in an online magazine that's read all over the world by tens of thousands of people.

Ahmed understood how it worked. All I had to do was log in with my username and password, type the words, "I have been kidnapped," click the Publish button, and everyone would know what had happened to me.

The United States government, though, officially refuses to negotiate with terrorists. That policy is sometimes ignored when convenient or necessary, but it didn't look good for me.

Would a protest movement break out in the United States on my behalf? I doubted it. Americans are far less likely than Israelis to think negotiating with terrorists makes any sense. And when Israelis mobilized for Shalit, they were championing one of their soldiers, a young man sworn to protect them. I'm not a soldier. I never served in the military. I'm a writer. A journalist. Most journalists are hardly better respected than members of Congress, whose approval ratings are barely in the double digits.

I get it. Journalists are biased. We're sensationalists. Foreign correspondents in particular have a habit of parachuting into obscure war zones for a week and acting as if they'd been able to discuss the finer points of the local politics ever since college.

Too many journalists want to change the world. That isn't me. Don't get me wrong: changing the world is great and all as long as that change isn't negative, but that isn't me. One of the main reasons I got into foreign correspondence is because I was working in a cubicle farm as a technical writer and desperately needed to get out of the office. I wanted to write something challenging and important, something that people actually wanted to read. I didn't want to spend my life cooped up in a cubicle or even a home office tapping away at a keyboard. I needed to get *out*, see the world, explore strange places that people don't visit on holiday.

Places like Iraq. Believe me, if you're a writer and you find that you're blocked, that you have nothing to say, go to Baghdad. You'll find plenty to write about if you go to Baghdad or some other blown-to-shit place. Winston Churchill once said nothing is so exhilarating as being shot at without result, and he was right.

In France during the riots of 1968, an anarchist spray-painted the following on a wall: "In a society that has abolished every kind of adventure, the only adventure that remains is to abolish the society."

I'm hardly an anarchist, but I've long understood the fear and loathing of the ennui that can suffocate people in settled societies. The human brain is wired for struggle and strife. If there is no struggle and strife in our immediate environment, some of us will go out of our way to create it. I can only imagine how much more tempting that impulse must have been for young people raised during the stultifying 1950s and early 1960s. The anarchists, however, were wrong. If you're bored with your life in the suburbs, there's no need to pick a fight with the country that raised you. Go to the Congo. Go to Somalia. Go to Iraq. You'll be walloped with as much struggle and strife as you can stand. You'll learn that, actually, there's a lot to be said for boring tranquility.

One night in Baghdad, while I was working as an embedded reporter with the United States military, an American officer asked me how I got into this job. I told him that I wanted to get out of the office.

He laughed and said he couldn't wait to *return* to the office.

We both laughed. I understood him and he understood me.

Now here I was, more cooped up than I'd ever been. Having a day job in a corporate cubicle farm is radical freedom compared with being held captive by terrorists.

Ahmed brought me some new clothes—a pair of Levis, some short-sleeved button-up shirts, some underwear, three pairs of black socks, and a pair of already-worn Nikes that were a half size too large. He also brought me a toothbrush, a tube of Crest, a bar of orange Dial soap, two towels, a black bottle of men's shampoo so I could wash my hair in the sink, and a sleeping bag. He did not bring me a pillow, nor did he bring me a mattress or cot. I'd still have to sleep on the floor, but at least I could pile up some clothes and soften things up a bit.

He also brought me the laptop, as promised. I poked around to see if I could enable a wireless Internet connection, but of course I could not. I had to check, though, just on the off-chance that he didn't know how to disable it properly.

I opened Microsoft Word. Ahmed said he would make sure that whatever I wrote appeared on my blog. But what was I supposed to say? In all likelihood, hundreds of thousands of people would read it. Now that I had been kidnapped, my writing would get more attention than ever.

That's great and all, but I also knew my mother would read it. So would my wife. Every one of my friends and acquaintances were going to read it. My parents would damn near have strokes if they hadn't already. My wife would collapse in despair. I knew this. Nothing I had ever written or said in my life would cause more pain and grief to the people I loved than whatever I was about to write next.

But I had to proceed. I'd seen enough parents of kidnapping victims on television say it was not knowing what had happened to their children that tormented them most. And if Ahmed was telling the truth, if he really would publish whatever I wrote without editing it, I could tell everyone I was fine under the circumstances and I could write it in such a way that everyone would know I really wrote it.

I composed the following entry:

> *I have been kidnapped by terrorists. They took me out of my house in the night and locked me up in a basement. The leader calls himself Ahmed. He says he was born in Seattle. I don't know if that's true, but he speaks English without an accent. His sidekick calls himself Mahmoud. He's a disgusting oaf of a man who grunts instead of speaks. He punched me once in the mouth, but otherwise I'm unharmed.*
>
> *There are at least two more upstairs who I haven't seen yet.*

I can hear them walking around and talking up there, though I can't quite make out what they're saying.

I assume everyone already knows why they kidnapped me so I'm not going to repeat it here. "Ahmed" says he has a "cause" and wants to use me to bring attention to it. Well, I'm not playing. He's welcome to schedule a press conference and tell you about it himself. He can hire a publicist or stand on a street corner and yell at cars. I don't give a shit.

Ahmed thinks the fact that I'm writing anything at all is useful to him, and no doubt that's true, but it's also useful to me. I need my family to know I'm alive.

If anything ever appears on this blog that looks like propaganda for Ahmed, rest assured that one of three things is happening. 1) I didn't write it. 2) They held a gun to my head while I wrote it. 3) I'm suffering from Stockholm syndrome.

I paused, unsure if I should write the next section. But he said I could write whatever I wanted, so I went ahead and wrote what I wanted.

I hereby give the FBI permission to raid this house with guns blazing if they figure out where I am, even if there's a chance that I'll get shot in the crossfire. Find me and take the bastards down with extreme prejudice.

I saved the file and stepped away from the laptop. I considered yelling up the stairs and letting Ahmed know I had something for him to publish, but why should I? I wasn't in a hurry to see him again and, anyway, he could wait. I had no intention to cooperate any more than I had to.

An hour later, while I was looking at the line of trees out one of the basement windows, he came downstairs to check on me. "Have you written anything yet?" he said.

I gestured with my arm toward the laptop. He opened it and pressed the power button.

"You're not going to like it," I said. "But you'd better publish it exactly as is if you want anyone to believe you didn't write it yourself. If you censor me or add any words of your own, people will know. Especially my family."

"We won't censor anything," he said. "We want everyone to know it's really you."

I watched his face as his eyes scanned the screen while he read. He flinched slightly when he reached the end, but then he smiled.

"This is perfect," he said.

"I didn't mention the prisoners in Guantánamo," I said.

"It doesn't matter," he said. "I've already taken care of that. Mahmoud called your local police department in Portland from a pay phone. He told them we have you and he told them why. He also called your local newspaper. The story has been picked up all over the country. All over the world, in fact. Every story I've seen so far mentions the prisoners we want released. Everyone in the world knows why you're here. We don't need you to write about that."

"How do I know you're actually going to publish what I wrote without censoring it?"

"I want you to trust us," he said. "So after we publish this, I'll bring the laptop back down and let you see it on your blog for yourself. By the way, do you realize how hard it is to find a pay phone these days? It took Mahmoud almost an hour."

"Where did he finally find one?" I said.

He gave me a fake smile. "Please," he said.

"Well," I said. "You've done a fine job concealing our location. All I know is we're somewhere in the Pacific Northwest. I think it's safe to say you didn't steal me away to Algeria."

He twitched ever so slightly when I said "Algeria." Was that where he's from? Did I guess right the first time? I only randomly mentioned Algeria, but on some level I knew that was a possibility. Some countries in the Middle East and North Africa produce more people like Ahmed than others. Egypt and Saudi Arabia are the biggest producers of political radicalism, but Algeria is another. And I could tell by looking at him that he wasn't Saudi. Neither was Mahmoud. They both looked Mediterranean. The bloodlines in North Africa and the Eastern Mediterranean are mind-bogglingly complex. A person from a place like Egypt, Lebanon, or Algeria could easily be a genetic composite of Arab, Persian, Greek, Spanish, French, Turkish, Italian, Armenian, and Albanian.

"You should know," Ahmed said, "that Mahmoud called your wife."

I caught my breath. Could that be true? How could he call her?

"I don't believe you," I said. "You don't have her phone number."

The truth is, I didn't believe myself. I didn't know how they would find her number, but it probably wasn't hard. They found out where we live, so why couldn't they get her number? I just hoped—desperately—that he was screwing with me.

"Of course we have her number," he said. "Finding it could not have been easier." He reached into his pocket and pulled out what looked like my iPhone.

I lunged at him and reached for it, but he was ready and he shoved me back. I could have punched him and grabbed it, but he knew I wouldn't, not with Mahmoud and the others only seconds away.

"How do I know that's my phone?" I said.

He turned it on and scrolled through the list of contacts. I saw my wife's name and the names of all my friends and close family members. I leaned forward and vomited onto the floor next to my shoes.

"She knows now what's happening," he said, "and she heard it from us. Your mother knows, too, but I told Mahmoud to leave her alone. For now anyway."

I gasped and spit on the floor, fearing I'd be sick again.

"I don't mean to torment you with this," he said. "Your phone has personal information in it, I know. It must be agonizing to see it in the hands of somebody else."

I hadn't felt so violated since the first night they took me. But I also felt the faintest flicker of hope. What if there was a way I could get that phone back? Sneak upstairs in the night, find it, figure out where I was with my phone's GPS, and call 911?

"So I'll do you this favor," he said and placed the phone on the floor next to his feet. Then he smashed the thing and twisted it into the concrete with the heel of his boot.

Chapter Four

I was curious what Mahmoud said when he called Shelly, but I was dying to know what she said back to him. Did she scream? Did she start crying? Did she demand they let me go? Did she beg?

The muscles in my neck were bunching into a knot, so I sat on the floor in a corner and rubbed my own shoulders while playing out one gruesome scene in my head after another. Unlike the parents of kidnapping victims, I decided that I actually didn't want to know what she said. But in my preferred scenario, my wife told them she hopes they get the death penalty. I'd been viscerally repulsed by capital punishment my entire life, but at least once an hour, when I wasn't fantasizing about killing Ahmed and Mahmoud myself, I liked to imagine them sizzling and popping on an electric chair.

These thoughts disturbed me. I didn't feel guilty of anything, exactly, but the sheer frequency of my own bloody fantasies couldn't be healthy. Was my brain being rewired forever? If I did manage to get out of there, would I ever be able to sever these dark loops in my mind?

But I stopped the moral hand-wringing the next time Ahmed came down the stairs. He brought the laptop with him and set it on the table. First he showed me that he had uploaded my blog post to the magazine without editing it, but that wasn't the reason he came down.

"There's something else you need to see," he said. "You should sit."

I sat and had no idea—no idea at all—what I was in for.

He used the touchpad mouse to open several folders. Then he hovered the pointer over a Windows Media file.

"You ready?" I said.

"I guess," I said.

He clicked the file and launched a video on the screen.

I saw a naked man lying on his back on a table with his wrists and ankles bound. Wires were attached to his nipples. Three uniformed men stood over him. I assumed they were soldiers. The vantage point appeared to be from a stationary camera installed in a ceiling corner.

"What is this?" I said and turned to look at Ahmed.

"Just watch," he said and nodded, his eyes on the screen.

I looked back at the screen and braced for what I was certain was coming.

One of the soldiers barked something in Arabic at the man lying on his back. The sound quality was terrible and I couldn't understand a word, though I was obviously watching an interrogation.

The man on the table sobbed and said "I don't know" in Arabic to the soldiers.

A barrel-chested soldier stepped toward the wall and flipped a switch. The prisoner screamed and arched his back. Even though the film quality was grainy, I could see that every muscle in his body was convulsing.

"Why on earth are we watching this?" I said. "Where was this filmed?"

"In Egypt," Ahmed said. "Nine years ago."

The soldier flipped off the switch and briefly put the prisoner out of his misery.

"That's Mahmoud," Ahmed said and pointed at the screen.

"Who?" I said. *"Him?"*

"Him," Ahmed said. "The big one." The one who was shocking the prisoner.

I never would have recognized him had Ahmed not said anything. Mahmoud was nine years younger in the video, clean-shaven, and a little less fat. But it was him, all right. Now that I knew, it was obvious.

"Why are you showing this to me?" I said.

"Just keep watching," Ahmed said.

The younger Mahmoud, the one in the video, barked something

again at the prisoner. The prisoner sobbed.

Mahmoud stepped out of view of the camera for a moment. Nothing happened on the screen for a couple of seconds. Then the prisoner shrieked as Mahmoud stepped into view again. He held something in his hand, but I couldn't tell what it was.

The prisoner knew, though, and screamed in sheer terror and pulled as far away from Mahmoud as his restraints would allow.

Then I saw what Mahmoud held in his hand. It was a knife. A long one, like a hunting knife or bayonet. He held it up to the prisoner's face and barked something again in Arabic. The poor man kept screaming.

So Mahmoud began cutting into the man's belly and chest.

I flinched and turned away from the screen.

"It doesn't hurt as much as you'd think," Ahmed said. "Not with that much adrenaline in his system. His screams are from fear as much as from pain."

I couldn't look, but I also couldn't block out the sound of the screaming.

"I need you to watch this," Ahmed said. He reached under my chin, grabbed my face, and forced my head back toward the screen. I didn't resist. This was no time to resist.

It went on for another thirty seconds or so, Mahmoud cutting and the prisoner screaming. Mahmoud finally stopped and barked another question in Arabic. This time the prisoner didn't answer at all, not even by shrieking or sobbing. Mahmoud slapped him. Still no response.

I was cold, yet I felt sweat running down my chest and my forehead. My adrenaline levels were spiking and my whole body tensed up.

"This next part is what I really need you to watch," Ahmed said.

My God, he was a psychopath. Both of them were. The man on that table was a human being, but Mahmoud went to work on him like he was a sheep being butchered for dinner.

On screen, Mahmoud stepped out of camera range again. And this time he came back with a drill.

"Oh God, no," I said.

"Watch," Ahmed said.

"I can't," I said.

"Watch!" he said.

I squinted at the screen and winced.

Mahmoud turned on the drill. The high-pitched whine was unmistakable even through the shitty laptop speakers. Then he plunged it into the prisoner's knee. The poor man snapped out of his stupor and screamed like nothing I'd ever heard in my life, like the pain was destroying his mind.

"That drill he's using is tipped with a blade," Ahmed said, "You can't see in the video, but it's there. There's nowhere near enough adrenaline in the human body to block that kind of pain."

"Turn it off!" I said. "Turn it off!"

"Okay," Ahmed said in a calm voice. "Okay."

He closed the laptop.

I just sat there and breathed, on the verge of hyperventilation, not saying anything.

"What do you think?" Ahmed said.

"What do you *think* I think?" I said.

"Was that disturbing?" he said.

"Of course it's disturbing," I said. "Fuck! Why do you have that on your computer?"

I knew I'd never get those images and sounds out of my head. Never. I was sure that was the point. But I needed to know. "Why did you show this to me?"

"I need you to understand," he said.

"Understand *what*?" I said. "What is there to understand about something like that?"

"Do you know what that man did?" he said. "The prisoner?"

"I have no idea," I said.

"Nothing," he said. "He didn't do anything. He was just an Islamist. That's why he was arrested and tortured."

I was shocked and appalled and more afraid than I had ever been in my life, but I still could think. Egypt's former President Hosni Mubarak lorded over the country with a military dictatorship, but it wasn't a sadistic police state like Saddam Hussein's in Iraq. His soldiers and police officers arrested and sometimes tortured members of the Muslim Brotherhood, but I'd never heard of them drilling into anyone's kneecaps. The man on the table was almost certainly more than just an Islamist. He was probably a terrorist, or at least suspected of being a terrorist.

"Why on earth," I said, "would Mahmoud torture a fellow Islamist?"

"He was in the army at the time," Ahmed said. "His political views hadn't matured yet. Unlike me, he was always a Muslim. But he hasn't always been an Islamist. His experience in the army clarified many things. I shouldn't have to remind you that after the Zionists, Mubarak was America's best friend in the region."

I took some deep breaths. Tried to slow myself down.

"What happened to that man?" I said. "To the prisoner."

"He died on the table a few minutes later," Ahmed said.

"Mahmoud killed him?" I said.

"When Mahmoud drilled into his other knee," Ahmed said, "he died of a heart attack."

"Jesus fucking Christ," I said.

I've always been comfortable with a certain amount of darkness in my life, as long as it's not my own personal darkness. I'm a foreign correspondent, after all, and sometimes that means I'm a war correspondent. Every day I spent in Baghdad I risked being blown to pieces by an IED or a car bomb. My buddy Noah Pollak and I hunkered down on the Lebanese-Israeli border in 2006 while Hezbollah fired thousands of rockets in our direction. In 2008 I took a train across the Caucasus from Azerbaijan to Georgia when Russia invaded.

No one was targeting me personally in those situations. Sure, I could have been killed, but I would have been a random casualty of war. No one from any of those places called and menaced my wife. And because

I was there voluntarily, I could head home the minute I'd had enough.

But I couldn't escape Ahmed's basement. I was no longer a tourist on the dark side. I was trapped in it.

Every time I heard the creaking of floorboards near the basement door, I wondered if that was the moment. Was it finally throat-cutting time? I couldn't stop staring at the stairs leading up into the house and imagining the door flying wide open and my killers descending.

I tried to convince myself that I should relax, that it didn't mean anything that I could hear them talking and walking around up there. Of course I could hear them. It didn't mean they were talking about me or were on their way down to cancel my ticket. But I couldn't stop.

I needed to bug out of there, but I couldn't break free, nor could I fight my way free. I ran my hands through my hair and thought about kicking the chair across the room, but I didn't want to make a giant racket, so instead I kicked the concrete wall with the flat of my foot.

I didn't study journalism in school. Never even took so much as a class. What I studied was fiction writing and literature. There are rules in fiction that don't apply in real life. An author can't, for example, place the protagonist into a plot corner he can't get out of without using his own skill, cunning, or strength. The hero in a novel can't be a passive victim who is simply acted upon. He or she can't be rescued by chance, by fate, or by God. Main characters can't sit around and wait for lightning to strike down the bad guys. A protagonist must face an antagonist, but he must ultimately be the author of his own victory or demise.

If I were writing a novel about a man who was kidnapped and thrown in a basement, I'd give him a tool to escape. His captors would make a mistake and leave an avenue open. He'd find a butter knife, for instance, and tunnel into a wall with it. And he'd have something to cover the hole with. Or he'd have a cell phone. Or something he could use as a weapon. He'd have something! But Ahmed left me with nothing.

Fiction is tidier than reality. It has to be. Otherwise it wouldn't work. But I wasn't a character in a novel. This was actually happening. I ran a thought experiment, though. What if this *was* a novel and I was the author? What would I have my character do? What fatal mistake had the bad guys made that wasn't obvious to them when they made it?

Well, Ahmed's entire strategy had a potentially fatal flaw right at its center. Forcing me to write was a brilliant ploy for attention, but it left me a line out to the world. Surely he'd delete anything I might say that would help the police find the house, but what if I could slip something past him?

The FBI had to be paying extremely close attention to whatever I wrote. But I'd have to be careful. I'd have to reveal something that would help the authorities without Ahmed figuring out what I was up to. But what? What could I say?

I took stock of what I knew. Ahmed's family was likely from Algeria, even if he wasn't born there himself. Mahmoud was in the Egyptian army nine years ago. They were holding me somewhere in central or eastern Washington state. Even though I could barely understand what they were saying when I heard them through the floorboards, I could tell they were plotting. Once I heard talk of money and "our next operation." Kidnapping me wasn't the only thing they were up to.

I needed more. I'd need to probe Ahmed for as much information as possible without his realizing that I intended to cryptically include what he said in a message out to the world.

Next time he came down, I'd be ready.

Great news, *habibi*," he said the next morning. "Don't call me that," I said. "We're not friends."

He ignored me.

"You're famous," he said. "Your story is on the front page of the *New York Times*. You're all over CNN, MSNBC, and Fox News. And so are we. I looked at your Web traffic statistics, and 250,000 people have read your blog post so far. Ten thousand people read it in just the past half-hour alone."

"Awesome," I said. "I guess."

The truth is, it was sort of awesome. My blog never had so many hits. Ahmed really had made me famous. I wondered if my books were selling more copies. And I was happy to think my wife must have read the message by now. She'd know I was alive, or at least that I had been alive recently. She knows me better than anyone. She'd know I wrote that post, that there's no way it was written by some dipshit terrorist. It had my personality all over it like dirty thumbprints.

"They're all talking about whether or not to release the prisoners from Guantánamo," Ahmed said. "They're debating it on Fox News right now. The host is saying the United States doesn't negotiate with terrorists, of course, but millions of Americans already thought the prisoners should be released. And they've thought so for years. If they do get released, and if we let you go, you'll have a blockbuster book on your hands. It will be a best seller."

Hatred welled up inside me all over again. For years I've had a dark fantasy about being kidnapped for exactly that reason. It would give me one hell of a story to write about. But I'd only want to be kidnapped if I could somehow know in advance that my time in captivity would be short, that I would not even be beaten, let alone tortured or killed. Now here I was, kidnapped and locked in a basement. I had already been beaten. I had been threatened with torture. They menaced my wife. And Ahmed used that dreaded word *if*. *If* they let me go, I'll have a blockbuster book on my hands. *If* they let me go means they might not.

If Ahmed had said *when* I get out alive, I would not have believed him. I knew what he looked like. I knew what Mahmoud looked like. I could identify them in an FBI lineup.

Had he said *when* I get out alive, I could have at least taken comfort in fantasy. But he refused to give me even that much. He wouldn't even pretend that he planned to release me and tormented me instead with that awful word *if*.

He came downstairs the next morning as I stood at a window and fantasized about escaping into the trees. He sat in one of the chairs.

"Come sit, *habibi*," he said.

I lingered at the window a few moments and made my way over to him with seeming reluctance.

"We should talk," he said.

"What could we possibly have to talk about?" I said. I did want to talk. I needed more information, but I could not let him know that.

"You are our guest," he said.

I snorted.

"So we should get to know each other better," he said. "Don't you think?"

"I already know everything about you that I need to know," I said.

"What do you think?" he said. "That I'm a terrorist?"

"Of course you're a terrorist," I said.

"Define *terrorist*," he said.

"I'm not playing this game with you," I said.

"Listen, *habibi*," he said. "I won't say I'm a freedom fighter. I wouldn't expect you to find that convincing right now."

A different tone crept into his voice all of a sudden, a tone less menacing and a little more honest.

"We're holding you captive," he said. "You deserve to know why. And I want you to know that I've never killed anybody."

I wanted a cigarette. I hadn't smoked in years, but I desperately wanted a cigarette.

A man I hadn't seen before padded down the stairs in his socks. He brought with him a teapot and two cups on a tray. He smiled warmly as he placed a cup in front of me and filled it nearly to overflowing before he even placed an empty cup in front of Ahmed.

I might have killed an innocent person right then if the universe would have rewarded me with a microbrew or a coffee, but tea would just have to do.

"Thank you," I said. And I meant it. He had a kind and gentle look about him.

"*Afwan*," he said. *You're welcome* in Arabic. "I'm Ismail." He reached out his hand to shake mine. After a moment's hesitation, I shook his hand.

He seemed a decent sort somehow. He was a terrorist and criminal, of course, and I was sure his friendliness was at least partially choreographed to manipulate me, but people have a certain energy about them even when they're wearing a mask, and Ismail's seemed benign. He could have been a friendly waiter in the neighborhood teahouse. I felt better with him in the room, even if it was just an act.

He filled Ahmed's cup also to near overflowing, left the teapot so we could pour ourselves more, and headed back toward the stairs.

"*Shukran jezeelen*," Ahmed said to him. *Thank you so much.*

Ahmed wiped his face with his hands and rubbed his eyes with his palms.

"I hate terrorists," he said. And it sounded like he actually meant it.

I looked at him and waited for him to say something else, but he didn't.

"You kidnapped me," I said.

"It's a criminal act," he said. "I admit that."

"And you're holding me here until the government lets almost two hundred terrorists out of jail."

"No," he said. "They are not terrorists."

"Oh," I said. "So you're not a freedom fighter, but *they* are?"

"They are guerrillas who were captured in Afghanistan," he said. "I won't insult your intelligence by calling them freedom fighters. I know they're with the Taliban and Al Qaeda."

If his objective was to emotionally whipsaw me, he was succeeding. Being trapped in that house with him was like living with a violent alcoholic. You never know which person just walked in the door—your loved one or the monster version.

"So if you hate terrorists," I said, "and you acknowledge that the Taliban and Al Qaeda aren't freedom fighters, what on earth are you doing? Why are you holding me here? Why do you want to get them released?"

"They are Muslims," he said, "and they were captured fighting an imperial power. The September 11 attacks were a despicable act, but the men you captured in Afghanistan are innocent of that crime."

"Who do you mean by *you*?" I said. "Do you mean Americans? You're an American. You were born here."

"I don't belong to this place," he said. "You guessed right about where my family is from. My parents are both from Algeria."

"I guessed lucky," I said.

"It was an educated guess," he said. "You're a smart man. I know that. You wouldn't be here if I thought you were stupid."

I started to chew on a fingernail. "Do you by chance have a cigarette?" I said.

"Ismail has some," he said.

"Do you ever smoke?" I said.

"Once in a while," he said. "Do you? I didn't know."

"I quit years ago," I said, "but I've been craving one since I got here."

He nodded. "Ismail!" he called toward the top of the stairs. "Bring us some cigarettes and some matches. And an ashtray."

Ismail came down the stairs with a crumpled package of Camels, a book of matches from 7-Eleven, and a ceramic ashtray with traditional sky blue North African designs painted on it. This time he wore shoes instead of socks, he smelled of tobacco, and the ashtray hadn't been used. He must have been smoking outside.

"Thanks, Ismail," I said.

"*Shukran*," Ahmed said and slid the pack toward me. Ismail padded back up the stairs.

I tapped a cigarette out of the crinkled pack and slid it back and forth under my nose. Burning cigarettes stink and full ashtrays smell even worse, but I'll swoon at the sweet aroma of unsmoked tobacco for the rest of my life.

"You know," I said to Ahmed, "Al Qaeda in Iraq shot people for smoking. They shot people in Fallujah and Ramadi just for having a cigarette."

He laughed and lit his cigarette with a match. "Such assholes," he said and shook his head. "I'm sorry. I shouldn't laugh. It isn't funny."

He leaned forward and lit my cigarette from the same match.

"But you're holding me captive until the government releases Al Qaeda guys who were captured in Afghanistan. You don't even make any sense."

"Al Qaeda in Iraq was led by Zarqawi," he said, referring to the deceased Jordanian psychopath Abu Musab al-Zarqawi. "He should have concentrated on driving the Americans out of Iraq. Instead he killed tens of thousands of Muslims."

He took a deep drag on his cigarette and tapped his ashes into the tray.

I took a drag, too, and was hit at once with such a powerful nicotine rush that I had to hold onto the table.

"How am I supposed to take what you're saying seriously?" I said. "If we were debating this in a coffee shop instead of—"

"Even Osama bin Laden found Zarqawi offensive and said what he did was counterproductive."

I couldn't argue with Ahmed about that. I spent some quality time in Fallujah and Ramadi in 2007—Iraqi cities that Zarqawi's thugs had briefly taken over—and I was shocked and appalled by what I saw there. Entire sections of each city had been pulverized into oblivion. I never saw any place in Baghdad that was even a fraction as wrecked as Ramadi. Mile-long swaths were just gone, simply erased, as empty as parking lots, the rubble and twisted rebar hauled away. The Al Qaeda creep jobs that took the place over were like gangs of Hannibal Lecters. They massacred civilians with car bombs. They sawed local teenagers' heads off with kitchen knives.

Americans who wonder why moderate Muslims don't stand up to extremists have never been to Ramadi. Al Qaeda ostensibly showed up in town to fight the American occupation, and many Iraqi civilians initially welcomed them for that reason, but their behavior was so unspeakably ghastly, so bloodthirstily fascist, that the Iraqis formed an alliance with the American soldiers they'd previously hated so they could purge their neighborhoods of that cancer.

The phrase *war on terror* always sounded hokey to me, and it still does, but it didn't sound the least bit hokey when I was in downtown Ramadi, a city of 400,000 people that was so chewed up by IEDs, air strikes, machine-gun fire, and car bombs that it looked like World War II had blown through the place.

"The Afghan warriors are more honorable," Ahmed said, "though I will admit that some of them are a bit ... problematic. But listen, *habibi.* The American empire must be resisted. It should not be, it cannot be, resisted by Muslims killing Muslims, nor should it be resisted by hijacking airplanes and flying them into skyscrapers. The Pentagon, of course, was a legitimate military target, though the civilian plane that crashed into it wasn't. American soldiers abroad are also legitimate targets. That's why they wear uniforms. It's what military uniforms are for. They say, in effect, Shoot me and not the civilians."

"I'm a civilian," I said. "And you took me out of my house while I was fucking asleep. You showed me Egyptian torture porn and threatened to cut off my eyelids. My fucking eyelids!"

I shouldn't have said it. He could sic Mahmoud on me whenever he felt like it, and there wasn't a damn thing I could do about it. I also needed information from him, information I could try to sneak out to the world next time he asked me to write something on my blog, if only I could figure out how. The last thing I needed was to get in a fight with him.

"If you want me to take you seriously," I said, "tell me honestly that you don't plan to kill me."

He stabbed out his cigarette in the ashtray. The basement smelled like a tavern now. I'd need to open the little windows to air the place out. I rubbed my own cigarette out, too, and suddenly detested myself for smoking it. My mouth tasted revolting and my fingers stank like a lowlife's.

Ahmed changed the subject.

"The mujahideen aren't freedom fighters the way you would think of a freedom fighter," he said. "They aren't fighting for gay marriage or to legalize marijuana."

I rolled my eyes. I couldn't help it.

"But," he said, "they are fighting for the rights of Muslims to live as they please in their own lands without American tutelage. They're a bit harsh for my tastes, I admit that. I wouldn't force women to wear burkas. A veil or even a headscarf is enough. But these are questions for we Muslims to work out for ourselves. You have no place in these discussions. And, truly, they are fighting for all of humanity. I don't expect you to understand this right now, but every human being is a potential Muslim. Every human being. All they need to do is read the Quran. To read the Quran, to be properly educated, and to just make an effort to know and love God."

The best thing, I knew, was to let him keep talking. He was revealing himself to me unprompted.

"I want to tell you a story," he said, "about my family." He wouldn't look at me now, choosing instead a point in space over my shoulder or on the wall behind me. "My parents are from Algiers. The capital. They left in the 1970s and came here."

"To Seattle," I said.

He nodded. "They're secular people. Atheists. They raised me and my sister that way. No one in my family is religious. My uncle, he stayed in Algeria. He was in the army. When I was in college, he—" Something seized in this throat. He swallowed hard and forced himself to continue. "He went into this village outside M'Zab. You know M'Zab? It's an oasis town in the Sahara eight hours south of Algiers. They said terrorists were holed up in this village—Islamic radicals that wanted to turn Algeria into another Saudi Arabia. The army is secular, of course. Fanatically and murderously secular like the Soviet Union. The soldiers went into the village. My uncle was one of them. And they burned the place down.

They raped women right there in the open. They threw grenades into houses where kids were taking shelter. They even butchered the animals."

I didn't know what to say. Algeria in the 1990s was one of the most horrific places on earth. One hundred fifty thousand people were killed there in the civil war between Islamist radicals and the communist-style regime.

Ahmed took another cigarette out of Ismail's package and lit it.

Oh, what the hell, I thought. My mouth was rancid already, and my fingers reeked of burnt tobacco. If I was going to have another cigarette, I may as well do it now before I washed my hands and brushed my teeth. So I reached for another cigarette, struck a match, and lit Ahmed's before mine.

"Shukran, habibi," he said.

I nodded.

What was this? For the briefest of moments I had forgotten that I hated Ahmed and that he had kidnapped me. He and I were connecting as human beings naturally do, even human beings who are adversaries. Part of my mind recoiled, but I forced myself to just go with it. He seemed to feel the same way, at least for a moment, and that made me safer.

I took a deep drag off my cigarette, exalted in the delirious head rush it gave me, and gently blew smoke out the side of my mouth away from Ahmed's face.

"A few years ago," he said, "my sister went to visit our uncle and some other family members who still live in Algiers. I don't know if she knows about what happened in that village outside M'Zab. No one in our family talks about it. I've never heard it discussed in my sister's presence. So she goes over there to visit and she takes a day off to drive in the mountains."

A feeling of dread washed over me, and I braced myself for what he would say next. I knew it wouldn't be good. At least his sister was still alive. He talked about her in the present tense.

"Don't drive in the mountains," he said. "That's what everyone in

Algeria says. The mountains are dangerous. So is the desert. So is the city. Every place in Algeria is dangerous, but especially the Atlas Mountains. My uncle says the mountains are full of terrorists. But no terrorist harmed her in the mountains of Algeria. She was stopped at an army checkpoint and forced to get out of the car. She went driving around by herself. Can you believe it? A woman driving around a Muslim country alone? And in Algeria of all places! She doesn't speak very much Arabic. She can order food from the menu, that sort of thing, but she can't talk her way out of trouble. She was born here like I was. She's an American. And when the army guys at the checkpoint found out she's American and saw that she was dressed like a Los Angeles stripper, it didn't even register that she's just as much an Arab as they are. They treated her like the slut they figured she was."

He didn't elaborate, nor did I ask him to elaborate. I could easily imagine rough men with guns throwing her against the hood of the car and yanking her pants down to her ankles.

"You know what's wrong with Algeria?" Ahmed said.

I didn't answer. I wanted to know what he thought.

"You," he said.

"Me?" I said, astonished. "I've never even been to Algeria."

"You," he said, "and your country and your kind. America supports the regime in Algeria just like America has supported every Arab dictator, including Saddam Hussein. America supported the regime in Algeria when it canceled the elections in 1991. Why? Because the Islamic Salvation Front came out ahead in the first round. You guys were so afraid of Muslims in government, and your buddies in Algiers were so afraid of Muslims in government, that 150,000 people had to die so you could make your point."

I could have argued with him. Algeria's government did cancel the elections after the first round, it's true, but the Islamists responded with a horrifically savage insurgency. Deranged mobs rampaged throughout the country, hacking people to death with machetes. Feminists, artists, journalists, foreigners, hairdressers, writers, anyone deemed even vaguely cosmopolitan or liberal was placed on hit lists. People like me, people like Ahmed's sister, were hunted down and exterminated. It was unspeakable. Algeria's government is like a creature hatched from a lab in the STASI's East Germany, but the Islamist reaction was so monstrous in the eyes of so many that one could argue—as many did—that the government, nasty as it was, was perfectly justified in not letting such people get into power, elected or not.

"I swear to you before God," Ahmed said as his hands shook, "that I will never do the kinds of things my uncle or anyone else in the Algerian army has done."

I had no idea what to say. He'd become so unpredictable. It was awkward, but I partly agreed with him. And God help me, but I felt like I was bonding with him at that moment. Was this the beginning of Stockholm syndrome? I wanted him to like and respect me. My life and my safety depended on it. And I wanted to like him, at least a little bit, and find some good in him so that I'd have hope that at some point he might let me go.

"I don't want to be here," I said.

"I know," he said and nodded sympathetically.

"So let me go," I said.

"You know I can't do that, *habibi*," he said. "Not while our comrades are still being held. Write something for your blog. I'll have Ismail bring the laptop back down."

He stood up to leave.

"Ahmed," I said.

He looked at me.

"Don't do this," I said.

"Don't do what?" he said.

"This," I said. "Don't keep me here like this. You want attention for your cause in the media? Let me go. Show the world you're better than the United States government. Show the world that you let your own prisoner go after less than ten days while Washington refuses even after more than ten years."

He smiled.

"That's clever," he said.

"I'm not trying to be clever," I said. "I'll write nicer things about you if you let me go. I won't lie. I promise you that I will not lie. I'll tell the world you were decent to me. I'll tell the story of what happened in that Algerian village."

He squinted. I could tell he was wondering if maybe he would score a public-relations point or two if he let me go without harming me further.

"And I'll tell the world what happened to your sister."

The muscles between his eyes tightened, and he kicked the chair across the room and sent it crashing into the wall.

"You will do no such thing!" he said. Then he picked up the chair and swung it behind his head like he was preparing to smash it into my face. "How dare you threaten to dishonor my family!"

I watched his face carefully, looking for more telltale signs of imminent violence.

"I didn't mean it like that," I said and leaned back to slightly increase the distance between us. "I apologize. I wasn't thinking."

His face and neck were both red, but he was relaxing ever so slightly.

"I shared that with you," he said, "so that you'll understand me." He set the chair down. "If my sister dressed properly, if she at least covered her hair if not her face, and if she took her Arabic seriously, she would not have been raped. She would have been seen as a good wholesome Muslim, a sister Algerian. Instead she acted like an American whore and got exactly what she deserved."

Chapter Five

Ismail brought my breakfast the next day. He started bringing all my meals to me, actually.

"Hey, man," he said when he saw me.

I picked up a vaguely hippie vibe from him and kept expecting him to say "dude." Maybe he was an ex-hippie who converted to Islam. People don't change their body language and general bearing after a religious conversion. I figured that even if Ismail was a pure sadist underneath a facade, I could still count him as a small blessing. I felt better when he walked in the room. Ismail the hippie dude may have been an illusion I constructed to make myself feel better, but it still made me feel better.

After lunch he brought the laptop. I would have been just as happy to see him as I had been at breakfast, but I was in a bit of a funk, still shocked by what Ahmed had said about his sister.

But of course the man who kidnapped me to free Taliban and Al Qaeda prisoners would think his sister deserved to be raped for dressing like a "whore" in a Muslim country. I was a fool for thinking he'd see it my way. I shouldn't have projected my psychology onto him.

On some level I was aware I was doing the same thing with Ismail, so I promised myself not to do or say anything stupid because of it.

How different from Ahmed and Mahmoud could Ismail possibly be? Unless he was an FBI infiltrator, he was one of them. And if he was an FBI infiltrator, I'd have already been freed. He wouldn't have let them kidnap me in the first place.

After he left me alone with the laptop, I opened Microsoft Word and stared at the flashing cursor on a blank screen, and it hit me. There *was* a way I could slip a secret message into a blog post, a message that the FBI might see and that Ahmed might not.

My online magazine had a feature I could exploit. The blog-publishing software used what's known as the WYSIWYG format. It stands for "What you see is what you get." If I wrote text in a Microsoft Word document that was italicized, and that material was copied and pasted into the publishing software, the text would be italicized when it appeared in the magazine. If I made the text red instead of black in Microsoft Word, and the red text was copied and pasted into the publishing software, the text would be red when it appeared in the magazine. If I changed the text color to *white* in Microsoft Word, and the white text was copied and pasted into the publishing software, the text would be white when it appeared in the magazine. And since the magazine used a white background like Microsoft Word does, the text would be imported and published, but it would be invisible.

I could write a message to the authorities in invisible text. Only the text wouldn't be invisible to everyone. It would only be invisible to most people. Anyone who looked at my blog with an RSS program like Google Reader *would* see the invisible text because RSS strips away the WYSIWYG formatting and converts all text to black.

Thousands of people read my blog through Google Reader or another personal online aggregator. All of them would see my "invisible" text. At least one of them would make sure the authorities saw it.

Ahmed, though, had no reason to read my blog that way. He had direct access and had no use for third-party software. So I wrote the following:

> *The bastards still have me and they're not letting me go. They asked me to blog again, but this time I hardly know what to say. Ahmed says he isn't a terrorist because he's never killed anybody. And he insists the prisoners he wants released aren't terrorists either because they were fighting a guerrilla war against the American military in Afghanistan. Yet they're holding me, a civilian, hostage.*

*I don't know where I'm being held, but it can't be that hard
to find me. If the president of the United States can zot terrorists
from the skies with Predator drones over Yemen and Pakistan,
how hard can it be to find a terrorist den in the United States?*

Come get me.

*And to my wife, my mother, my father, my brother, and all
my best friends: I love you all and miss you like I've never missed
people before. I miss you more than I thought it was possible for
human beings to miss one another. I'd like to tell you not to worry
about me too much, but I know that's impossible. Just know that
they aren't hurting me (really, they're not) and that I fully intend
to get out of this.*

*And to Shelly: please pet our cats for me and tell them I love
and miss them. I love you and miss you more than anyone.*

Then I wrote the following and changed the color of the text from
black to white so Ahmed wouldn't see it but everyone using an RSS
reader would.

*Washington state. East side of Cascade mountains. Isolated
house in pine forest. Ahmed from Seattle via Algeria, Mahmoud
served in Egyptian army, another named Ismail, plus an unknown
fourth man. I'm in the basement. Terminate everyone on the
main floor.*

I considered mentioning Ahmed's video of Mahmoud torturing
someone to death, but thought better of it. I wanted the FBI to know
about it, but I did not want my wife and mother to know I was at the
mercy of someone like him. So I censored myself.

"I have another blog post for you," I said to Ahmed the next time he
came down. I blinked a few times, swallowed hard, and hoped he didn't
notice. It was too late to back out now. "Remember, you promised not to
edit a word. Just click 'Select all,' then copy, paste, and publish."

I couldn't look at him.

"We won't edit your work," he said as he took the laptop upstairs. "We've already been over this."

I knew if he discovered the second, hidden part of the message, I'd be beaten or worse, but I had to do something. I promised myself I'd fight my way out of that house if I had to. Break the glass out of one of the little windows and cut each of their throats, including Ismail's, one at a time as they came down the stairs.

My phone was destroyed, but I had to talk to my wife. I couldn't take it anymore. I couldn't eat and couldn't sleep at all the night before. I physically ached for human contact, and it took everything I had not to cry.

So I sat down on the floor, looked into space, and talked to my wife.

"I don't know when I'll be home, but I love you, Sweetheart." I knew she couldn't hear me. I wasn't losing my mind. I just had to say it. "I miss you, but I'll see you soon."

I was getting used to sleeping on the poured-concrete floor. It hurt, of course, and at first I woke up once an hour to move so the pressure would dig in somewhere else, but it wasn't all that different from sleeping on a backpacking trip. Sleep just hurt now. It was one of those things. I told myself my back would feel better when I got up and stretched in the morning. I eventually got to the point where I could sleep for almost two hours in a row instead of one, and I was in a deeper sleep than I had been in a while when Ahmed raged at me the next morning.

"You!" he hollered as he flung open the door at the top of the stairs.

I was aware of him doing this at the edge of my consciousness, but in my dreamy state I had forgotten what I'd done the previous day. And my fear of him had ebbed somewhat after our last conversation. I groaned and covered my eyes in a vain attempt to get back to sleep.

I heard heavy footsteps as he came down the stairs, and I snapped awake at the sensation of danger.

"Get up!" he yelled and I felt a powerful slug in my stomach. I grabbed my belly and gasped for air. The bastard had kicked me.

I rolled over from my side to my back and struggled to breathe, but my abdominal muscles had completely seized up. Ahmed stood over me like a tyrant.

"We know what you did," he said. He towered over me with his legs planted wide and flexed his fingers.

I was finally able to blow the air out of my lungs and take a deep breath.

"I don't know how you did it," he said, "but I know what you did."

I just lay there and looked at him with my hands over my stomach and my chest rising and falling.

"Get up," he said and cocked his foot like he was preparing to kick me again.

I sat up. This was no time to be confrontational, but I had to say something.

"Wouldn't you try to escape if you were me?" I said and winced in pain.

"Of course," he said. "It's your job to try to escape. And it's my job to not let you."

He kicked me again, this time in the ribs. At least I was fully awake and could brace for it.

"Mahmoud," he said toward the top of the stairs. "Come on down."

Mahmoud clomped down the stairs slowly in those work boots of his. He carried a drill bit in his hand. A drill bit with a bladed tip.

"Mahmoud has very simple instructions," Ahmed said. "You try one more stunt like that and he's taking your wife. He's going back to your house, and he's taking your wife."

My heart leapt into my throat and I felt my whole body flush. Even though I was sitting down, I had to place the palms of my hands on the floor to keep from falling over.

"What were you thinking?" Ahmed said. "You know we know where your house is."

Mahmoud spun the bladed drill bit between his index and middle fingers.

I realized then that I was hyperventilating and that my pulse rate must have doubled.

"In the meantime," Ahmed said, "you've lost your privileges."

Mahmoud went into the bathroom and confiscated my towels, toothbrush, toothpaste, and soap. He scooped up all the clothes that I wasn't wearing. Then he clomped his way back up the stairs.

"Do you know why I showed you that video?" Ahmed said. "That video of Mahmoud when he was in Egypt?"

I had an idea.

"Tell me," I said.

"To illustrate a very simple point," he said.

I just looked at him.

"Pain is an instrument," he said. "It's a tool. It isn't the only tool, but it's a tool. It's like a blowtorch or a hammer. It has no moral dimension. The Egyptian army uses it. The Taliban uses it. The United States government uses it. Most important for you, Mahmoud uses it. I don't care for it myself, but Mahmoud even used it for a cause he didn't believe in."

On his way out of the basement, he slammed the door like a gunshot.

Chapter Six

I didn't see Ismail again for a while. Mahmoud brought my meals now. He narrowed his eyes and stared holes through me every time he approached with my tray. He wasn't going to bring breakfast and kill me at the same time. I knew that. But still. I could tell by the look on his face that he wanted to kill me. The only reason he didn't was because Ahmed wouldn't let him.

He brought me prison food, basically, which I supposed was appropriate. Breakfast was an egg boiled extra hard and white bread without butter or jam. Lunch was a sandwich made with the same cheap crap bread and a paper-thin slice of turkey. No cheese, no mayo, or anything else came on that sandwich. Dinner was two small pieces of cold and overcooked chicken. They gave me no fruit or vegetables. They sure as hell didn't give me coffee or tea. When I was thirsty, I drank water directly out of the bathroom faucet.

I spent a whole day sitting on the floor and leaning against the wall and staring into space. I wasn't allowed to have the computer, of course. Who knew what other kinds of trickery I might try to pull off?

Part of me missed running in the park each evening and my twice-weekly martial-arts class. I had a vague notion that I should do push-ups and stomach crunches to keep myself fit and to give myself something to do, but what I really wanted to do was go numb for a while. I wasn't eating much and had lost a few pounds, but I didn't want them to know that, so I flushed whatever I didn't eat down the toilet.

Would Mahmoud really go after my wife? He might if he and Ahmed thought it would make me compliant. The administration of pain is a tool, Ahmed had said, and would be used whenever it's needed. If they'd use it against me, why not my wife?

But she would be much harder to find. They knew where she lived, of course, but I was certain she'd left the house after what happened to me. She and I have friends and family all over the country she can stay with. We have friends all over the world, actually, from Europe and South America to the Middle East and East Asia. She lived in East Asia for a while before we were married. For all I knew, she'd gone back there where no one could possibly find her.

The inside of my mouth tasted disgusting. I could bathe in the sink even though I no longer had a towel to dry off with, but you can't clean your mouth with just water. I desperately needed some toothpaste. I've been told the Lebanese penal system won't let prisoners have toothbrushes. I don't know if that's true, but it struck me as medieval after I'd been deprived of one myself for three days. How primitive man made it through life without toothpaste, let alone dentistry, escaped me.

But Ahmed took mercy on me and brought my toothpaste back. He didn't bring me anything else, but at least he brought that.

"We should talk again, *habibi*," he said.

"Don't call me that," I said and snatched the toothpaste from his hand. "I'm not your friend."

"It doesn't always have to be like this between us," he said. He sounded sincere, like he actually wished that I liked him.

"Let me go and we can have a different conversation," I said.

"It's important to me that you understand something," he said.

"Hang on," I said. "I'm going to brush my teeth with my finger."

I stepped into the bathroom and turned on the water, expecting him to continue speaking, but he waited. I vigorously rubbed mint Crest on my teeth and sucked every last dollop of the stuff off my finger. I saw him sit on the floor out of the corner of my eye as I swished warm water around in my mouth.

I spit out the water, licked my deliciously clean teeth, took a deep breath, and looked at myself in the mirror. The downside of establishing a rapport with him was that I might succumb to Stockholm syndrome.

The upside of establishing a rapport with him was that it would be harder for him to kill me. Despite the risk, I had to forge a relationship with him that transcended the prisoner-kidnapper dynamic.

"Come sit," he said when I emerged from the bathroom.

"Don't you want a chair?" I said.

"The floor is fine," he said.

He leaned up against a cobwebbed wall near a corner. I sat and leaned against the same wall a few feet down. We didn't look at each other. Just stared straight ahead.

"You have a right to understand why this is happening," he said.

"We've already been over this," I said.

"I don't mean what's happening to you personally," he said. "I mean everything. Why we do what we do."

"Can I ask you something first?" I said.

He nodded.

"How did you find out?"

"Find out what?" he said. "Oh, that. I have to admit, sending that message was clever. They were talking about it on TV."

"Who was talking about it?" I said.

"It was all over the news."

Sometimes I truly detest my media colleagues. Did it never occur to them that my captors watch television?

"Some bloggers found and copied your message," he said. "The news said they found it with an RRS or whatever."

"An RSS reader," I said. "Real Simple Syndication. Like Google Reader."

"I understand why you did it," he said. "It's in your nature to try to escape. And I respect that. I just need to do a better job ensuring you can't. You can't very well escape with toothpaste, though, so you can keep that."

I was tempted to say thanks, but I resisted. He owed me a lot more than toothpaste.

"I should have known you'd come up with something," he said. "Half of you guys are spies anyway."

"Half of what guys?" I said and resisted rolling my eyes. I knew what he meant. I'd heard his "theory" dozens of times, if not hundreds, while working in the Middle East.

"Journalists," he said.

"I'll tell you what I tell everyone else who thinks I'm a spy," I said. "My Arabic stinks. I'll never understand Middle Eastern societies like the people who've lived there their whole lives. Our CIA agents were born over there. They're the ones who can penetrate the government and steal secrets. I don't know anything secret. I'm a white guy from Oregon. I don't know a single thing the CIA doesn't already know. Our agents over there are military officers and businessmen. Government advisers."

"You said, *our*," he said.

"I said what?"

"You said *our agents*."

"Oh, for god's sake," I said. "I meant America's agents. I'm an American."

"You could be a case officer," he said, "who recruits local people. Journalism is a great cover. It gives you the perfect excuse to set up meetings at ministries of foreign affairs."

"It's against the law," I said, "for American spies to use journalism as cover."

"That's what makes it such a great cover!" he said.

There was no beating him at this. To the conspiracy theorist, every piece of evidence against the conspiracy reveals another layer of the conspiracy.

"Is this what you wanted to talk about?" I said.

"No," he said. "I want to talk to you about Sayyid Qutb."

My veins ran cool, even icy.

"You know who he is," he said.

I knew. And he knew that I knew because he could read it on my face.

"I know who he is," I said. "Or at least who he was."

Sayyid Qutb is to the terror war what Karl Marx was to the Cold War. He was born in Egypt in the early twentieth century and joined the Muslim Brotherhood as an adult. While starting out as a relatively "moderate" Islamist, he later gravitated toward the fanatical wing of the movement and wrote thousands of pages of political and Quranic philosophy. Perhaps one of the reasons hardly any Westerners have ever heard of him, aside from the fact that his work isn't widely published in English, is because it's nearly impossible for non-Muslims to sympathize with him. Certain kinds of Westerners can find Marx and Engel's *Communist Manifesto* compelling, but none would feel a gravitational pull toward Sayyid Qutb's *In the Shade of the Quran.*

"You know about his experience in Colorado then?" Ahmed said.

"Of course," I said.

Qutb spent a bit of time in Greeley, Colorado, in 1948 at the university there. The experience changed him, and not for the better. Most foreign students who study abroad in America tend to appreciate the United States more than they did before they arrived, but not Sayyid Qutb. Qutb was horrified by America. He detested the place as a den of sin and iniquity. He reeled at the sight of unmarried women and men dancing together in public.

"And what do you think of his take on America?" Ahmed said.

"He was a knee-jerk reactionary," I said. "He found the United States excessively libertine in the 1950s? Give me a break."

"I agree," Ahmed said. "He was reactionary. But he was only reactionary because he was describing America in the 1950s. What about America now? Almost half the children here are born to unmarried women. All anyone thinks about is the pursuit of pleasure and the avoidance of pain. Drugs, alcohol, sex, loud music, adultery, gambling—the country is rife with it. This place is the id of humanity."

"Have you ever been to Algeria, Ahmed?" I said.

"Of course," he said. "It's even worse there than here. Algeria was lost so long ago, there's hardly anything left to go back to. It was lost when the French colonized it two hundred years ago."

"I don't want to live anywhere but here," I said. "Not anymore. I've been there and done it. At least America, for all its faults, is a free country. Singapore is cleaner, safer, and no one does drugs, but it's like living with control freaks for parents or in a museum where you're not allowed to touch anything."

"The solution," Ahmed said, "is not a police state that controls everything. That's the American way, or at least the American way abroad. You support the regime in Algeria just like you supported the regimes in Egypt, Tunisia, and everywhere else. Islam is the solution."

"But the religion of Algeria is Islam," I said, "and you yourself said it's in worse shape than America. So how is Islam the solution?"

"Islam in Algeria is not the solution," he said. "The solution is Islam in America."

I paused. That was not what I was accustomed to hearing, not even from radical Islamists.

"You want to convert America to Islam at gunpoint?" I said.

"Not at gunpoint," he said. He turned toward the stairs. "Ismail!" he hollered. "Please bring us some tea, *habibi.*"

So I was allowed to see Ismail again. Good. I hated even the thought of Mahmoud coming downstairs again. Even if Ismail's general pleasantness was part of some elaborate good-cop-bad-cop routine, that didn't change the fact that I felt relieved when he walked in the room.

I heard footsteps in the kitchen above. If I could just sneak up there and take one of the knives out of the drawer ... but of course they wouldn't have any sharp knives in the drawer. Not where there was a chance I could reach them.

"There is no compulsion in religion," Ahmed said. "You know that's what the Prophet Muhammad said, may peace be upon him. No one will convert you or anyone else at gunpoint. Islam calls all of humanity. It's the fastest-growing religion in the world. Christianity is dying. Judaism barely took off to begin with. The Jews don't like converts. It makes our job easier."

The idea that America would ever become Islamic—especially red states like Texas—was absurd, but I didn't say anything.

"Not until hundreds of years after the Arabs conquered the nations of the Middle East and North Africa," Ahmed said, "did the majority of the population convert. Lebanon held on with an outright Christian majority until the middle of the twentieth century. God is patient, *habibi*. So are we."

There's no chance *I'll* ever convert to Islam. I was baptized Catholic, raised Protestant, and am now thoroughly secular. If I ever do decide to return to religion, it will be to the one I was given at birth, whose holidays I still celebrate and whose culture I'm firmly a product of.

"Sayyid Qutb looks like a reactionary to us," Ahmed said, "but only because he was ahead of his time. You know what else he had to say about America."

I nodded.

What Sayyid Qutb said about America was not good. It was not good at all. His ideology was the driving force behind Al Qaeda's declaration of war on America.

Qutb believed Christianity is grotesquely flawed, not so much because it isn't Islamic but because it's too liberal and secular. The separation of religion from government, he believed, was embedded in the religion itself at the very beginning. "Render unto Caesar the things which are Caesar's and unto God the things that are God's." That's what Jesus supposedly said during the time of the Roman Empire, and it's in the Bible. Christianity, then, was doomed from the start to suffer the remorseless encroachment of "Caesar" and every other imaginable form of government secular human beings would dare to design, from liberalism to communism and fascism.

Qutb believed moral decadence rots secular societies from the inside if religion is banished to its own corner, that secular societies are rent asunder by what he called a "hideous schizophrenia." Christians go to church on Sunday but live hardly any differently from atheists the rest of the week.

The problem with all this for Sayyid Qutb, and his acolytes like Osama bin Laden, is that America is a superpower that exports its ideas. America exports its culture and its values to the rest of the world. The moral corruption that made Colorado of the 1950s so revolting to Sayyid Qutb has spread across the world from the United States like an oil slick. Christendom's hideous schizophrenia was infecting Cairo.

The Egyptian government hanged Qutb in prison, but the process of Americanization, so to speak, continued after his death. With the collapse of the Soviet Union, the United States stood unopposed. The Middle East was looking and feeling more like the morally repulsive West every day. Arabic music videos shot in Beirut are more sexually suggestive by an order of magnitude than anything that ever appeared in conservative 1950s America. If Qutb could see it all now, he wouldn't wait to be executed. He'd hang himself.

"If America was a Muslim country, the world would have a Muslim superpower," Ahmed said. "Do you think if the world had a Muslim superpower that we would see half-naked women on Arab beaches like we do now? Do you think the Palestinians would not have a state? Do you think a monster like Moammar Qaddafi could have ruled Libya for so many decades? Would we have a communist-style government in Algeria?"

"You're blaming America for communism now too?" I said.

"Not entirely," he said. "The Algerian regime was a Soviet ally. I'll give you that. But the United States supports it now to prevent Muslims from coming to power. So you are also responsible."

"So you're telling me," I said, "you want Americans to convert to Islam and export the Quran instead of liberalism and capitalism."

"Yes," he said.

"And that's why you've kidnapped me."

"No," he said. "I'm giving you the big picture. Telling you the long-term plan. In the meantime, your country must be contained. America is more resilient than the Soviet Union. The martyrs in Afghanistan won't bring you down. We understand that. But your imperial ambitions must be contained. It may take 1,000 years before a Muslim man sits in the White House, and that's fine, but until then every American soldier who steps even a toe outside the U.S. will be a target."

"You think American soldiers on a joint training mission in Canada ought to be targets."

"Yes," he said.

"Really." I said. "In Canada."

"It's like this," he said and leaned forward. "If it's okay for American soldiers to conduct missions in Canada as guests of the government, what's to stop American soldiers from conducting missions as guests of the government in Algeria, Egypt, Iraq, and Afghanistan?"

"Ahmed," I said.

"You see where I'm going with this?"

"Ahmed."

"No," he said. "You listen."

I clammed up. I really did want to know what he had to say. He was exposing the engine that drove him. It drove everything that was happening to me and around me.

"This will play out one of two ways," he said. "America will retreat to its own borders and slowly convert to Islam. Or America as you know it will be destroyed."

I just sat there and blinked at him, slightly in awe of his extremism and delusion.

"Listen, *habibi*," he said. "I am a moderate. Destroying America is not what I want, and anyway what I mean is that America will no longer be what it is now. It will become like post-Soviet Russia. Because the United States as it is constituted today is an existential threat to Islamic civilization. Egypt is more degenerate now than America was when Sayyid Qutb studied abroad in Colorado. You've been there. You know! It's worse. Have you been to the nightclubs in Cairo? They are appalling! At the rate things are going, Egypt will be as atheistic as Sweden in less than one hundred years."

"Ahmed," I said.

"Stop," he said. "Just understand something. Your country is an existential threat to my civilization. How does America treat existential threats to *its* civilization?"

I didn't want to answer that question.

"Osama bin Laden declared war against America as a first resort," he said. "As a first resort. For me, it's a last resort. But if even moderate people like me think you'll need to be destroyed if you do not change, then change is coming, *habibi*. It's coming."

Ahmed was no moderate. Moderates in the Muslim world are the ones who go to those nightclubs in Cairo he hates. Moderates in the Muslim world back secular parties and campaign for human rights. I know them. Some of them are my friends. Many of them have been murdered by people like Ahmed.

The planet is no longer big enough for people like Ahmed and me to coexist without clashing.

"So that's it," he said. "That's what this—that's what all this—is about. I just thought you should know. You will be resisted. In Afghanistan and everywhere else. Our brothers will be released from your jails. And do you know what else?" he said.

"What?" I said.

"One day the flag of this country will be pulled down," he said. "The stars and stripes will not forever fly over Washington. No flag lasts forever. None ever has. The next flag of this country will have a full moon on it. Your fifty stars and thirteen stripes only represent you. The moon is universal. It shines the same light over all of humanity so that all of us can see in darkness."

And with that he got up and left me. He had a bounce in his step as he went up the stairs. He clearly felt better. I, however, did not.

Muslim countries all over the world have flags with a crescent moon on them. The Turkish flag, the Tunisian flag, Pakistan's flag, and many others are emblazoned with a crescent.

The only one with a full moon is the flag of Al Qaeda.

Chapter Seven

I refused to stay in that house any longer. Every threat-detection system I had in my brain screamed that Ahmed would kill me if I didn't get out of there, and that he'd do it soon.

Before I went to Baghdad the first time, I mentally rehearsed some scenarios. The crucial one involved kidnapping. If anyone wanted to force me to go anywhere, either on foot or in a vehicle, they'd have to shoot me. Drawing a gun and ordering me to get in a car would not be sufficient. They'd actually have to shoot me. Because nothing—and I mean nothing—is worse for an American than being kidnapped by Al Qaeda.

I couldn't waste time on a long plan now that I was no longer useful. The United States government would never agree to a prisoner exchange, and now that Ahmed would not let me blog anymore—what *other* stunts might I be able to pull?—I'd become dead weight. A liability. A pain in the ass. It was fight-or-flight time.

The only reason I didn't break a window and start swinging glass shards is because Ahmed revealed a serious weakness, an Achilles heel in his mind, that I could exploit before having to fight my way out.

He was paranoid. He had a conspiracy theorist's view of the world. Conspiracy theorists always think their enemies are more powerful than they really are.

It hit me at once. I knew what to do.

Instead of me fleeing them, what if I could get them to flee me?

Thank you, Ismail," I said when he brought my breakfast the next morning.

I had scrambled eggs, butter for my toast, and a steaming cup of tea. Why were they being nice again? I suspected it wasn't because Ahmed was less angry at me than before.

"You're a mensch," I said to Ismail.

"A mensch?" he said as he set down the tray. "What's a mensch? Something good, I hope?"

"It's a Jewish word for a good person," I said.

He blinked.

Actually, it's a Yiddish word, which isn't exactly the same thing, but I wanted to screw with him.

"I thought you were Christian," he said, looking confused.

"I'm not Jewish," I said. "It just seemed like the right word for you somehow."

He frowned.

"Hey, listen," I said quickly and quietly. "We need to talk."

"You want to talk to Ahmed?" he said and turned toward the stairs.

"You and I need to talk," I said. "And we need to talk quietly. I need to tell you something important."

"What is it?" he said in a level tone of voice.

"Shh," I whispered. "Quietly. The others can't know."

"Why can't the others know?" he said, quieter this time.

"It will be bad for both of us if they know," I said.

He looked toward the stairs again, then back at me. He scratched his beard and whispered, "What is it?"

"First," I said and shielded the side of my mouth with my hand, "I need to know I can trust you."

"You can trust me," he said. He looked sincere. I hoped that he wasn't.

"I'm telling you this for your own good," I said, "so don't blow it. You'll suffer a lot more than I will. Okay?"

"Okay," he said and looked around the room as though something with fangs might leap out of a corner. "What?"

I took a deep breath. "Give me a second," I said. "It's not easy for me to say this."

He pursed his lips and looked around dartingly again.

"Maybe we should sit down," I said.

I sat on the floor. He sat directly across from me.

"Is everything okay down here?" he said.

"Yes, it's fine," I said. "Look. Ahmed is on to me."

"You mean the thing you did with your blog," he said.

"No," I said. "That was just a diversion. I mean he's *really* on to me. This isn't going to last very much longer."

He looked up at the ceiling as though he were trying to see through the floorboards above.

"I don't think Ahmed is planning to kill you, if that's what you mean," he said.

"No," I said. "It's not that. I'm not the one who is about to get killed."

His face sank and his mouth went slack.

"He's not—"

"No," I said. "He's not going to kill you or anyone else. Ismail." I paused again for effect. I needed him to think what I was about to say was one of the hardest things I'd ever said. It was, actually, just not for the reason I wanted him to think. "Ismail, I work for the government."

He gasped, stood up, and turned toward the stairs.

"Shh," I said and motioned toward the floor. "Sit down, let me explain."

He slowly sat down again, farther away from me this time.

"I mean," I said, "I really am a journalist. But sometimes I've consulted with the government. I don't work as a spy or anything, but I have debriefed the CIA."

His eyes bolted wide open. I felt a flush of terror, as well, now that I'd said it. We shared that moment together, both of us terrified for entirely different reasons. Nothing would be the same again, not for either of us.

They could kill me for what I'd just said even though it was bullshit.

I've never debriefed the CIA. I didn't even know anyone at the CIA. I've never met a single one of their agents, not knowingly anyway. But there was no taking that lie back. And I knew if Ismail were to run up the stairs before I could say anything else, Ahmed would send Mahmoud downstairs with his Leatherman or a pistol. So I had to speak quickly.

"They know where I am, Ismail," I said. "I had a tracking app on my phone."

He put his hand over his mouth. "Your phone."

"You guys took my phone from my house when you grabbed me," I reminded him.

"I had it in my pocket on our way over here," he said. He looked like he wanted to move but couldn't, as if someone had nailed him down to the floor.

"It had a GPS tracking app on it," I said. "Or at least it did before Ahmed smashed it with his boot."

"Then why—"

"I don't know why they haven't rescued me yet," I said, "but it's probably because they're putting together evidence for the other stuff you guys are doing."

"You know about that?" Ismail said.

I nodded.

I had no idea what else they were doing, though I assumed it was some kind of criminal enterprise. They might have been planning acts of terrorism in the United States, but no one had blown anything up lately, so they couldn't be guilty of more than planning something like that. They had money for a house in the woods and food for all of us to eat even though none of them had day jobs, at least not anymore. Where did they get the cash?

He should have seen through me. If the government really did know where I was, I would have been rescued at once, but I trusted I could make these guys sufficiently paranoid that they wouldn't think of that. Paranoiacs and conspiracy theorists can't convince themselves that threats to their safety are smaller than they appear. They have the opposite problem.

"The government isn't going to wait very much longer," I said, "now that Ahmed is on to me."

"I have to tell them," Ismail said.

That's exactly what I hoped he would do.

"No!" I said forcefully, but still quietly. "I'm telling you this because you have to get out of here. The FBI will come here and kill all of you. I'm telling you this because you have always been nice to me. You're a decent person, Ismail. Go. Leave tonight and go alone. If you try to flee with the others, the FBI will take you out too. Leaving now on your own is the only way you can save yourself. I owe you that much at least for the kindness you've shown me."

"I—"

"Just go, Ismail. Go with God."

He ran his hands through his hair, and I could tell by the look on his face that he wasn't sure what to do. I assumed his loyalty to the others would win and that he would tell them. I hoped all of them would bolt in the night and that I could walk out of the house free and clear. My odds weren't great. It was a desperate move on my part. But my only other option was trying to fight my way out, and that was a horrible option.

Ismail did tell the others, but they didn't react at all in the way I had hoped.

Two hours later. It was not even lunchtime. Voices upstairs in the kitchen. Whispering voices, but angry. Curses in Arabic.

I'd moved the chair to the center of the room, near enough to the stairs that I could swing wide and hit anyone who came down. If they charged down intending to kill me, I'd know. It would be obvious. You don't have to be an expert in body language to read violent intent. My odds would be terrible if it came to that. My odds would be even worse if they all came down at once. I was getting out of shape from being cooped up and not exercising, and I had only the bare minimum of martial-arts training, but I did have an advantage: I was ready for them.

The door at the top of the stairs flung open. "Michael!" Ahmed called from the kitchen. "We're leaving."

I didn't answer. What did he mean? Were they leaving without me? Most likely not, but it was possible. Or did they want me to go with them?

"Michael!" he said again.

"Mmm, huh?" I called out in a confused tone of voice, as though I had just woken up. I bit down hard on the inside of my cheeks.

"Get up here," he said. "We're changing locations."

He did not want to come down and get me. He sounded a little afraid of me now. He knew I might have something planned. It must have occurred to him that I had the table and chairs. But if he was worried I'd swing the chair at his head, why didn't he come downstairs with a gun? I hadn't seen any guns yet, but surely they had them.

"Michael!" he said. "Now."

"I hear you," I said in as even a tone as I could muster. "Where are we going?"

"To the other house," he said.

They couldn't have another house. Could they? Not like this one. They might still have places in Seattle, but why on earth would they have another isolated house out in the woods? Unless they had another hostage somewhere. Was I about to have company?

"Give me a second," I said. "I need to get my stuff."

He ran partway down the stairs and knelt so he could see into the basement. He saw me standing in the middle of the room and warily flicked his eyes toward the chair, then back at me.

"Come on," he said in a calm tone now that he could see me. What had he expected? That I was waiting down there with a flamethrower?

He wasn't armed. I didn't move. If he came all the way down and into the basement, I could bash in his head with the chair. The others would come down after him, including Mahmoud. I'd be in serious trouble. But it would be three to one instead of four to one. My odds were terrible, but they were not zero. If I followed Ahmed upstairs, though, my odds *would* become zero in any kind of a fight. I didn't even know the layout up there, and I was unarmed. So I froze.

"Mahmoud," Ahmed said.

Mahmoud slowly descended two-thirds of the way down and stopped. He carried a Glock 30 in his hand. And he just stood there with it at his side, the business end pointed down, a little more than twenty feet away from me. I couldn't rush him without getting shot.

This was exactly the situation I had rehearsed in my mind when I went to Iraq, when I swore it was better to be shot than go anywhere with kidnappers. The only difference was I had already been kidnapped. I had no way out. Waiting to be shot was pointless.

"All right," I said and raised my hands in surrender. I was done.

Mahmoud narrowed his eyes at me. Ahmed just stared. As I approached the steps, both of them backed up into the kitchen. Mahmoud never took his eyes off me.

The low ceiling forced me to duck my head as I climbed the stairs. I could finally see into the kitchen. It hadn't been remodeled in decades. The floor was faded yellow linoleum, the oak cabinets battered. Amazingly, the 1950s-era refrigerator still worked, because it was humming. Mahmoud leaned against the chipped porcelain sink.

Stepping over the threshold felt like crossing a frontier into another country. I'd been in that basement for so long, nearly ten days, that it had become my universe.

Mahmoud kept his finger on the Glock's trigger. I kept my eyes on him so I'd know the instant he decided to point that thing at me.

"Let's go," Ahmed said. "Outside and get in the van."

Ismail sat hunched over on a tattered brown couch in the living room and stared at his feet.

I heard Ahmed and Mahmoud come up behind me and felt the sting of a slap on the back of my head.

"I don't know if you're telling the truth about your phone or if you're full of shit," Ahmed said. "Either way, you're getting new accommodations. And you're not going to like them."

I stepped out onto the porch. The spicy scent of pine overwhelmed me. A soft wind blew through the trees beneath an overcast sky. The breeze on my face was as refreshing as a cool shower. Outside was room temperature. A perfect day for hiking in the forest—or fleeing if I could just get away. But how could I get away? Mahmoud would shoot me in the back. All I could do was get in the van.

Mahmoud jabbed the nose of his Glock into my spine. The van door slid open. Inside was the fourth guy, the one I hadn't seen yet. He was shorter and wirier than the others. He wore a thin shabby beard, the kind teenagers like to grow when they want to look manly before it's their time. He had rat eyes and the kind of mouth that never smiles. Of the four, he looked like the easiest to take in a fight. Maybe that's why I hadn't seen him yet. They needed Mahmoud to intimidate me, Ismail to play the good cop, and Ahmed to tell me what's what. That little rat bastard of a terrorist just looked like a punk.

I stepped into the van and Rat Bastard slid the door shut.

"You wear this," he said and handed me a burlap potato sack, "on your head."

Chapter Eight

I could hardly breathe with the sack over my face, and we drove for hours. No idea where we were going or even in which direction we headed.

Were they taking me somewhere to kill me?

No, I thought. They could have done that back at the house. It was isolated enough. No one would hear gunshots or screaming. If anyone did hear gunshots, they'd assume someone was hunting or shooting at cans. That's what people with guns do in the forests of the Northwest. I hear gunshots all the time when I go hiking and camping and it doesn't even occur to me that someone is shooting at people.

We couldn't be on our way to Seattle. In a city, all I'd have to do is scream and someone would hear me. They were driving with a purpose, so they had to have someplace in mind, but I had no intention of finding out where it was. If we stopped for gas this time, I'd run. Better to risk getting shot while running away with other people around than out in the woods or—worse—in the desert.

My face was burning up from the potato sack. My whole body was hot, but especially my face. Water vapor from my breath had condensed on the inside and soaked it. I tasted salt, and I couldn't stop licking my lips.

For the longest time no one said anything, but finally Ahmed said the words I was longing to hear.

"How are we doing on gas?"

I could tell from the direction of his voice that he sat in the passenger seat. I could smell the potatoes that had once been in the sack as it heated up.

"We'll need more soon," Ismail said from the driver's seat.

That meant Mahmoud and the little rat bastard were watching me in the back.

"Pull over here," Ahmed said. "And *you*," he said. I knew he was talking to me. "Shut up and stay in the back, or Mahmoud has orders to shoot you."

I felt the van slow down. Would they really shoot me in public? They might. I was certain, however, that they were far more likely to shoot me wherever they were taking me.

This was my moment.

I heard Ismail get out of the front seat and swipe a credit card. And I wondered: What's the name on that card? Was Ismail his real name? Was that card even his?

He stuck the nozzle into the tank. A few moments later, the gas started flowing. This was a van. The tank had to be huge. I'd have at least a couple of minutes to play this thing out.

"I need to get out," I said.

"You're not going anywhere," Ahmed said.

"I need the bathroom," I said.

"You can piss in the trees once we get going," he said.

"I'm going to throw up," I said and gasped. "Driving around with this thing on my head is making me sick."

He didn't say anything. I made a gagging sound and raised my hands to my mouth, though I kept them outside the bag so Mahmoud didn't think I was trying to take it off.

"Keep it together," Ahmed said. "We've stopped, for crying out loud. How can you be having motion sickness now that we've stopped?"

I keeled over, made more gagging noises, and, quickly as I could, reached inside the bag and jammed my finger in the back of my throat.

The rest took care of itself.

"You've got to be kidding me," Ahmed said.

"Ewww," Rat Bastard said. "He's throwing up on the floor."

Actually, I didn't throw up much. I just gagged. But it did the trick.

The van door slid open.

"Get him out of here," Ahmed said.

Someone lifted the bag off my head, and I squinted at all the sudden light. I saw a yellow-striped highway. A boarded-up café across the street with an old covered wagon out front. Sagebrush on low hillsides. Haze in the distance. No other cars at the station. The air was warm and dry. We were far from the ocean, in the Old West part of the state.

I stumbled out of the van, still squinting hard.

"Go with him!" Ahmed said quietly but firmly.

I hurried around the van, clutching my stomach as though I might throw up again at any moment. I did feel slightly queasy from gagging myself and from the odor of gas fumes, but I wasn't sick. I felt refreshed, actually, since I could finally breathe.

I felt a sudden burst of manic energy and ran toward the mini-mart attached to the station as a young women in her twenties walked toward me. She wore a red vest and looked like she worked there. A middle-aged man, perhaps her boss, stood and talked on the phone in a little office.

I looked at the woman and silently mouthed the words *help me.* Mahmoud was right behind me, no doubt looking sinister as all hell. She flinched at the terror on my face. She gave Mahmoud a double-take, and fear washed over her own face.

She understood me. Mahmoud might have known what I was up to, but he had to keep himself busy with me, not with her, and he couldn't very well yell out to Ahmed what I'd just done without blowing everything.

The woman walked past me and past Mahmoud as I headed toward the office and the man on the phone. What was she doing? I needed her to go in the station and call 911. Maybe she had a cell phone?

Gasoline was still coursing through the hose and into the tank. I still had a few moments before Ahmed would insist I get back in the van, but Mahmoud was right behind me. He would not let me out of his reach. I wouldn't be able to get inside and ask for help from the manager. So

I made gagging noises again, reached into my mouth, and plunged my finger in one more time.

"Come on!" Ahmed said.

Mahmoud shoved me hard in the back. He had to know by now that I was screwing around, but he was reluctant to manhandle me too much in front of people.

But where was that woman I had just silently asked for help? And where the hell were *we*? I saw more sagebrush than trees and didn't recognize the shapes of any of the low mountains on the horizon. We were in a nondescript part of the state that I either couldn't remember or never had any reason to visit.

I'll never know what that woman did during the ten or so seconds after I mouthed the words *help me*. Maybe she ran behind the van to check out the license plate. Maybe she was freaked out and needed a moment to figure out what to do.

But as I stood there and yakked onto the pavement with a looming Mahmoud gearing up to drag me back by my hair, she bolted past, ran straight into the office, said something to the man on the phone, and pointed outside.

Mahmoud pushed past me.

No, I thought.

The gas-station manager looked outside at the van, made brief eye contact with me, then slammed down the phone in a panic when he saw Mahmoud charging.

I saw him lift the receiver again and punch something into the phone. Mahmoud raised his Glock.

The young woman, in full-blown panic mode now, darted out of the office and into the mini-mart as Mahmoud pulled the trigger. The shot rang in my ears and punctured a hole through the glass. The manager dropped to the floor and knocked over his chair on the way down. The young woman screamed and ran into the back of the store.

"Mahmoud!" Ahmed yelled from the passenger seat.

"What's going on?" Ismail said, sounding panicked. He was still around on the other side of the van and hadn't seen a thing that led up to the shot.

Ahmed got out of the van as Mahmoud ran hard and fast into the store.

"'Mood!" Ahmed said.

The young woman screamed as Mahmoud barged through the door.

"'Mood, leave her be!" Ahmed said.

Mahmoud knocked over a rack displaying cheap sunglasses.

Ismail and Rat Bastard were both out of the van now and standing next to Ahmed. I thought about running, but I had nowhere to go. We were out in the desert. No place to hide. And there were no other cars on the road that I could flag down.

"She's seen our faces," Rat Bastard said quietly.

Ahmed stood beside me, and I saw that he had a gun in his hand. I instinctively reached for it. I had no plan. I just reacted. A woman in the garage needed saving, and I needed to get the hell of there.

To successfully disarm a right-handed man, you need to grab and force his gun down with your left, lock your elbow hard and tight so your arm won't bend when he tries to take the gun back, lean into him hard, and punch or palm-strike him in the face with your right. This will be the punch of your life. If you fail, he will probably shoot you. After throwing the punch, grab his gun with both hands and *twist*. His finger will snap if it's in the trigger guard. Even if it's not, you will have full control of the weapon and can pull it away from him.

I had practiced that maneuver hundreds of times on a mat, but in class my opponent was always standing in front of me. Ahmed was standing beside me. I had never practiced it that way, so I botched it. He pulled away before I could lock my elbow and push my weight into him, and he raised the gun and pointed it right at my eyes.

Three gunshots rang out in the mini-mart, followed by the sound of clattering boxes and plastic. Mahmoud killed the young woman. If I ran, he'd kill me, too.

"'Mood!" Ahmed yelled. "We need to move!"

Mahmoud stormed out of the store with his Glock aimed straight at my face.

"No!" Ahmed said and stepped in front of me. What was this? He was protecting me even now?

Mahmoud shoved him aside with both hands and pointed his pistol at me again.

I put my hands in the air and backed up until the side of the van stopped me.

"Mahmoud!" Ahmed shouted. "Stand down!"

Mahmoud lowered his pistol, but he did not slow down or lower his gaze. He stared into me with a molten hatred I'd never seen before, not even in movies. It was a hungry animal hatred, primal and instinctive and id-driven.

I didn't even see his fist coming my way. I just felt my face cave in like I'd been struck in the head with a bat, followed by nothing but black for minutes that stretched out like days.

PART TWO

"THERE IS NO COMPULSION
IN RELIGION"

Chapter Nine

I awoke in a wooden chair with my hands cuffed behind me and my head covered again with that sack. My world was darkness and pain. The left side of my face throbbed in agony. I braced myself, expecting to be beaten, kicked, burned, stabbed, or shot.

"Michael." It was Ahmed. "Do you realize what you've *done*?"

I struggled to free myself from the handcuffs. It's an instinctive response. You'd do it too. The mind needs proof that the body really is trapped.

I kicked my legs outward and felt something hard, most likely a gun barrel, jabbing into my ribs. I didn't know who was prodding me with that gun, but I heard him breathing. Most likely it was Mahmoud or Rat Bastard. It couldn't be Ismail. Could it?

"What do *you* think we should do with you?" Ahmed said. He was pacing back and forth. I could hear the soles of his shoes on hardwood.

I didn't answer.

"I still say we dump him out in the woods," Rat Bastard said into my ear as the gun barrel pushed harder into my side. "He's useless, and now we're in trouble."

Ahmed practically spit out his next words. "You don't work for the government."

That's not what he thought that morning. Why else did we hightail it out of the house?

"No," I said and breathed deeply. "I don't work for the government." I thrashed again. It couldn't be helped. I hurt and I desperately needed that suffocating sack off my head. "You killed people." I was grinding my teeth, and my jaw ached.

I didn't see Mahmoud shoot the girl. I just heard the shots. But I knew that he killed her. I didn't see the manager's body either, but I did see him fall.

"No," Ahmed said. "You killed those people."

"Fuck you," I said. A blow glanced off the right side of my head. Whoever hit me couldn't aim through the sack. It hardly hurt, though I likely would have been knocked right back out again if I'd been punched where Mahmoud had already hit me.

"Mahmoud didn't have to shoot them," I said.

Nobody said anything.

"You know it too," I said. "You yourself told him to stop."

"It was self-defense," Ahmed said. "They'd seen the van and had a look at our faces. You're the one who put them in danger. Don't try to put this on us."

"What about the security cameras?" I said.

"There weren't any," he said. "I checked before we left. That's the only reason we didn't burn the place down."

"They were innocent people," I said. "Innocent human beings."

"They were casualties in a war," Ahmed said in a hardening voice. "How many civilians have been killed by Americans in Iraq? How many hundreds murdered from the skies in Afghanistan?"

"Since when is the Pacific Northwest a war zone?" I said.

"It was them or us," Ahmed said. "And when it's them or us, I choose them every time. Don't tell me you wouldn't kill for your freedom."

"I wouldn't kill innocent people," I said.

"How many Iraqi babies have been killed to lower the price of your oil?"

I wanted to say something, but didn't. I wanted to say lots of things.

"You think you're so superior," Ahmed said. "So *righteous*." What sounded like a ceramic bowl and a tin spoon crashed into a wall and clattered onto the floor.

They were going to shoot me and bury me in the woods or the desert. I could feel it. There are millions of places in the Northwest to hide bodies where they'd never be found.

"Time to get rid of him," Rat Bastard said. "No one knows where he is. No one knows he's with us."

Listening to terrorists debating whether or not to kill you as if you aren't sitting there tied to a chair is … a unique experience. It does things to the mind. I tried to make myself small and invisible. I even felt slightly invisible on some irrational level. Since I couldn't see them with the sack over my head, a small part of my mind reasoned that if I didn't move, they might not see me and might even forget I was there, like I was a scared little kid pulling the blankets up.

"We might find a use for him," Ahmed said.

"And what use would that be?" Rat Bastard said.

"I don't know yet," Ahmed said.

I felt a hard slap upside my head, most likely from Rat Bastard. Why couldn't Ismail be in charge? And why didn't he say anything? I couldn't trust him. I knew that. If he was actually a nice person, he wouldn't be with this crew in the first place. But he was less unpleasant than the others, and I desperately needed to like and identify with somebody. I needed the world to be a fair and just place. I needed hope. A rock to cling to even if it was moss-covered and slippery.

"Tariq," Ahmed said. Tariq? Was that Rat Bastard's name? "You and Ismail go into town. Get a deadbolt for the bedroom and bars for the windows."

Rat Bastard sighed. God help me if I ever end up alone with him.

"And you," Ahmed said to me. "You need to understand some new rules. We got this place at the last minute. We're not as isolated as before. If you scream, there's a chance that someone might hear you. That's not an invitation to scream. If anybody shows up here, even if it's the police, this cabin is the last thing they'll ever see. Do you understand me? Two people are already dead, thanks to you, so if you care about anyone but yourself, you'd better shut up."

I started to protest, but he cut me off.

"Even if you *don't* care about anyone but yourself, if you scream,

Mahmoud won't kill you. I'll do it myself."

"I get to play with him first," Rat Bastard said. I couldn't see, but I imagined him grinning. And I heard the unmistakable sound of a thumb flicking across the sharp edge of a blade.

Mahmoud hauled me into another room, and Ahmed lifted the hood off my face. I was stunned to find myself in a pleasant vacation cabin. The place was decked out with high, timbered ceilings, expansive windows showcasing a cathedral-like evergreen forest beyond, fir floors so polished I could see my reflection, and wood and leather mission-style furniture that looked antique and brand-new at the same time. They must have rented it by the week or even the month. We had to be near a ski resort, a cool mountain lake, or at least some choice fishing holes.

They stuck me in a small bedroom on the ground floor, installed a deadbolt so they could lock me inside, and placed bars on the outside of the windows. I had my own private half bath, a luxurious bed with four pillows, and even my own climate-control knob on the wall. I could only think of one reason we hadn't just turned around and gone back to the first house. We must have crossed a state line. They had to cross a state line because two people were dead back at the gas station. We were in Oregon or Idaho or maybe Montana.

The room was a major upgrade from the basement at the last place, but I couldn't enjoy it. With nowhere to go and no one to talk to, I had far more time in my own head than was healthy. My own head was a bad place to be.

Two people really were dead because of me. I knew on some rational level that I wasn't responsible. Mahmoud pulled the trigger. I wouldn't go to jail for the crime. He would. Even Ahmed tried to stop him, which frankly surprised me.

But I didn't *feel* like I wasn't responsible. Had I kept my mouth shut, the young woman and the manager at the gas station would still be okay.

I'd be in better shape too, more likely than not. Rat Bastard might still want to kill me, but he'd have a much weaker case.

I didn't even know the names of the dead. They knew I was in trouble and they risked their own lives to save me, but I did not know their names.

My throat thickened up. I couldn't sit still in that room. I tried sitting on the bed, lying on the bed, and lying on the floor, but I couldn't get comfortable, so I paced back and forth. What I wanted to do was run until I collapsed.

I wondered where the woman at the gas station was from. Did she grow up in the Washington area? What about the manager? Did he own the place? Or was he just scraping by in the Northwestern outback? Did either of them dream of better things? A new life in Seattle or Portland, perhaps? Maybe they hoped to own and work land out there and live more aesthetically pleasing lives than employment at a gas station could ever provide.

I kept playing the scene over and over again in my head. What could I have done differently? What *should* I have done differently? I could have pulled the gas hose out of the tank and doused Mahmoud with it. He would have set himself on fire if he pulled the trigger. Or maybe I should have shut up and gone quietly to this cabin or wherever else they had planned for me, since it's where I ended up anyway.

I sat on the bed and heard Ahmed and Rat Bastard arguing in the front room. They tried to keep it down, but they didn't try hard enough.

"We can't stay here," Rat Bastard said, his voice just above a whisper but still audible.

"I know," Ahmed said quietly.

"He's useless," Rat Bastard said.

I felt hot and glanced at the window, but of course it was still barred.

"Maybe," Ahmed said. "Probably, but not necessarily."

"We have other things to do, you know," Rat Bastard said. "Sometimes it seems like all you even care about anymore is Guantánamo. We're nowhere near quota this year, and until we get rid of him, we aren't going to be."

"Don't you remember," Ahmed said, "how much trouble it was to get him here in the first place?"

Ahmed didn't say anything else. He really didn't know what to do with me. That was not good. As far as I could tell, he was the only one who wanted to keep me alive. Ismail rarely said anything. Mahmoud, I was sure, wanted to kill me, and Rat Bastard could hardly shut up about it.

I wanted to plead my case, to find some way to be useful to them even if just temporarily. There was always a chance I might be rescued, so the longer I could delay the inevitable, the better my chances were.

Who were they renting this cabin from? Did they do or say anything that made them look suspicious to the person who owned it? Maybe he'd come around, see that they'd installed bars on the outside of my window, realize something was fishy, and call the police before Ahmed could stop him. Maybe he already had called the police. Maybe my rescuers were only five minutes away. But what if they were five minutes away and Ahmed intended to kill me in three?

I knocked on the door.

"What?" Ahmed impatiently said from the living room.

"Can you open the door, please?" I said softly. "Just for a second."

He unlocked the dead bolt and flung the door open. "What do you want?" he said.

"I need to understand," I said. "I know I might not be around very much longer. And I need to understand. I need—"

"Ismail," Ahmed said.

"Yeah," Ismail said. It sounded like his voice came from the kitchen.

"Go into town and get Michael here a Quran in English," Ahmed said. "It's time he got himself an education."

He just stood there and stared at me. I saw Rat Bastard behind him on the couch squinting at me with hatred. Mahmoud sat quietly next to Rat Bastard and smiled.

Ahmed returned a few hours later with a Quran and two rubber kitchen gloves.

"You need to wear these when you handle it," he said.

"Excuse me?" I said. I knew why he wanted me to wear gloves. Fanatical Muslims think nonbelievers should not even touch a Quran lest they contaminate it. I should have just gone along, but I've never been the sort to roll over, and I had to say something. I opened my mouth, but Ahmed cut me off.

"Look," he said. "I don't care if you touch it. No one here but Mahmoud cares if you touch it. I got my fingerprints all over mine before I converted, and I don't think God minded. But Mahmoud will be offended." He paused to let that sink in. "So just wear the gloves."

I nodded. "All right," I said. "Thank you."

He handed me the gloves. I put them on and took the book from him.

"Read it slowly," he said. "Absorb every word. Open yourself up and let it flow into you."

"I will," I said. "Thank you again. I really do want to understand."

He left me alone. I felt ridiculous in the gloves and didn't know how I was supposed to turn the pages with them on my hands, but thought it best not to take them off yet.

I'd read parts of the Quran before, though not all of it. I felt duty-bound to read it since I worked in the Middle East as a foreign correspondent, but I don't write about theology, and I quickly realized that what's written in the Quran wasn't teaching me nearly as much about the Middle East as it actually exists in the real world as I thought it would. The book is more than a thousand years old. It was written in classical Arabic, an ancient language that some kids learn in school but no one speaks every day. Most people who self-identify as Muslims have never read it.

Muslims in general adhere more closely to their religion than Christians do, but the Quran doesn't have much bearing on how the average Middle Eastern person goes about his or her daily life. I was living in Beirut when I started reading it, and I realized in no time that the Quran was hardly teaching me more about Lebanon's people, culture, and politics in the twenty-first century than the Bible would teach Muslims about twenty-first century Miami, a city that Beirut resembles. So I put it aside and promised myself that I'd finish it later, a promise I only half intended to keep and might never have kept, had I not been kidnapped.

I read the whole thing in that cabin. My captors—especially Mahmoud, apparently—took the Quran a lot more seriously than my neighbors in Beirut did. I had nothing else to do anyway. More importantly, I figured they were slightly less likely to kill me while I was reading their holy book.

It doesn't take long to read anything while you're holed up in a room without distractions, but I pretended to read slowly, that I was only getting through fifty or so pages a day, that I was letting each word enter my soul one at a time.

Two days after I started reading the book, Ahmed checked on me in my room. I had become paranoid about Mahmoud barging in and seeing me holding the Quran without gloves on, so I kept wearing them while handling it despite the fact that they made my hands sweat.

"So what do you think?" he said.

"About the Quran?" I said.

"Yes, about the Quran," he said and smiled.

"I started reading it once before," I said, "years ago, and it had a strangely intense effect on me. It made me nervous, so I set it aside. I'm feeling it again, though it doesn't frighten me this time."

"You weren't ready before," he said. "I felt something similar the first time I read it, but I was ready."

"It's not like other books," I said. "Not even the Bible. It's like a powerful voice is reading the words aloud to me inside my own head. It's hard to explain."

I felt nothing like that while reading it, but Ahmed must have felt something when he read it, so he was inclined to believe the Quran would have a similar effect on me.

"For every step you take toward God," he said, "God takes two steps toward you."

"I'm not convinced it's God," I said. I had to be careful not to overdo it. I couldn't let him know I was yanking his chain. "It could just be stress and how overwhelmed I feel by everything that has happened."

His face sagged a little, and he sat next to me on the bed.

"Michael," he said. "Don't listen to your mind. Your mind will distract you with all sorts of rationalizations. Listen to your heart. What does your heart tell you?"

"I don't know," I said. "I'm confused. But I will keep reading and learning."

He wouldn't opt to kill me now, would he? It was his duty to spread the Prophet Muhammad's message to unbelievers, and I was all ears. At least I pretended to be.

"I would like to take these gloves off, though," I said.

He laughed and put his hand on my shoulder.

"Take them off then," he said, "when you aren't reading. Rest. Relax. Meditate on the words. And if you have any questions, if you don't understand something, just ask."

"I will," I said. "Thank you, Ahmed." I was surprised at how sincere I sounded when I said that. But I died a little inside. Whenever I looked at him, that young woman's screams at the gas station played in my head.

I lived and breathed at his pleasure. If the others wanted me dead (did Ismail want me dead too?), it didn't matter. Ahmed's word was law in that cabin. But I still wanted to soften them up. If they weren't so hell-bent on shooting me in the forest, maybe they'd stop pressuring Ahmed to just get it over with.

I never saw Rat Bastard. I only heard him once in a while out in the living room. Often he wasn't even on-site. He and Ismail kept taking the van into town—wherever "town" was—to pick up supplies. I wondered what else they were doing out there. They spent six to eight hours a day away from the cabin working on something. But what? With all the trouble I'd caused, I doubted they were looking for any more hostages. Were they looking for targets to bomb? Ahmed said they weren't terrorists, that they were only interested in resisting the American military abroad. But why should I believe him? Kidnapping me made him a terrorist. And he said he wanted to see the Al Qaeda flag—though that's not what he called it—snapping in the wind over the White House.

As far as I could tell, Mahmoud never left the cabin. He was Ahmed's security detail. If I tried to run or fight my way out, he was the one who would take care of it.

And Ahmed still used Mahmoud to intimidate me. He tasked Ismail with feeding me when he wanted me to relax, while Mahmoud brought my food when Ahmed wanted me nervous. Despite the fact that I was reading the Quran, Mahmoud was still the one bringing me meals.

I decided to try something. Since Ahmed found my interest in religion convincing, perhaps Mahmoud would, as well. So one morning when I heard him in the kitchen preparing my breakfast, I got down on my knees like I was preparing to kneel in Islamic prayer. When I heard him unlock the deadbolt, I slowly stretched myself on the floor like I was starting to pray toward Mecca.

He gasped when he opened the door and saw me. What I was doing had an effect, then, but what kind of effect? Was he happy to see me praying? Or was he offended that I was acting like a Muslim without first converting to Islam?

He knelt next to me and gently placed his hand on my back.

"Morning prayer has already passed," he said. I lifted my head off the floor and looked at him. These were the first words he had ever said to me. "Noon prayers will be in two hours. And Mecca is this way." He gestured with his open hand toward the barred window, about 45 degrees to the right of where I was facing.

"Thank you," I said. "Can you tell me when it's time?"

"I will tell you when it's time," he said.

He sounded so kind. So gentle. His voice was actually soothing. I could hardly believe he was the same brute who had shot two people just a few days earlier. After all this time, all I had to do to get on his good side was take a few steps toward becoming a Muslim.

What exactly was going on here? I was deliberately screwing with them, but then again, they put a Quran in my hands and had me prostrate on the floor. Who was manipulating whom?

"I will teach you how to pray properly," Mahmoud said, again in that startlingly kind-sounding voice.

"That would be wonderful," I said. "I don't really know what I'm doing. And honestly, I'm surprised to find myself trying. But I do want to try. It just feels like what I should do."

He came back a few hours later and told me it was almost time to pray.

"Prayer is called *salat*," he said. He showed me how to kneel properly, and he told me what to say.

Allahu Akbar. God is great. *Subhana rabbiyal adheem.* Glory be to my Lord Almighty. *Sam'i Allahu liman hamidah, Rabbana wa lakal ham.* God hears those who call upon Him; Our Lord, praise be to You. *Subhana Rabbiyal A'ala.* Glory be to my Lord, the Most High.

Then we faced Mecca together and prayed at the same time. I botched the words a bit—it's much harder for me to memorize phrases in Arabic than in English—so Mahmoud sat next to me on the bed and went over them with me again.

He even sang part of the Quran to me, and he did it from memory.

The Quran is meant to be sung rather than spoken or read. If you get into a taxi in the Middle East and your driver is religious, there's a decent chance he'll have the radio turned to a station that broadcasts the singing of the Quran twenty-four hours a day. I may be an infidel, but I have to admit that it sounds beautiful and makes a small part of me wish that I were religious. Professional Quran singers have a high, lilting voice that carries people away from the stress and the crowds and the noise of the twenty-first century. Middle Eastern cities can be exceptionally stressful and crowded and noisy—and none more so than Cairo, where Mahmoud was supposedly from. A man singing the Quran creates a blissful aural oasis.

I'll never forget when my friend Sean and I were traveling around North Africa in a rented car and we stopped at a little museum in the Atlas Mountain town of Le Kef in Tunisia, near the Algerian border. An unofficial guide near the Kasbah took us into an ancient chamber with a soaring ceiling and told us the room was for prayer.

"Do you know how we know this room is for prayer?" he said.

I had to admit I did not.

"Because our voices echo inside," he said. I noticed then that our voices were, in fact, echoing in the room.

And then he sang the Quran in a voice so clear and angelic, it sounded like he had come to us from another world. Sean was just as impressed, and he recorded the man's beautiful, haunting voice on his iPhone.

Mahmoud's singing was softer. He wasn't belting it out from his diaphragm, nor were we in an echoing prayer room. But the instant he started singing, he took me right back to the ancient room in Tunisia. I felt, for the briefest moments, a warm glow.

At the same time, another part of my mind kicked up a warning. That warm glow was dangerous. These guys were terrorists and criminals. And Mahmoud was once a professional torturer for Hosni Mubarak.

I wasn't foolish enough to believe they'd let me *go* if I simply went through the motions and made the right noises, but I was at least buying time. Time enough to maybe get rescued. Time enough to figure out another move later. Time enough to at least enjoy my view of the forest before they whacked me.

And time enough to be sucked even deeper into a dark world I had only begun to penetrate.

Chapter Ten

Ahmed came in beaming the next day. "I hear you're praying," he said. He looked relaxed, radiant even. I'd never seen him like that before. For the first time I noticed his laugh lines and how white his teeth were.

"I'm learning how," I said. "It's hard to remember the words."

He sat next to me on the bed.

"I had a dream last night," he said, "after Mahmoud told me what you're doing in here. I was deep in the desert south of Algiers. You rode on a horse to meet me and asked me to witness your conversion to Islam."

"I'm not ready for that yet," I said. "I still have a lot to learn."

"It took me a while," he said. "For the longest time I wasn't sure. My parents. I knew they wouldn't approve. And, of course, they didn't. And they still don't. I was twenty-two when I converted. I wish they knew God, but they don't even try."

"It's a big step," I said. "But I feel something when I read the Quran. I don't feel it all the time, but I feel it sometimes. Like the words have this … resonance, like the molecules in the room are vibrating with the rhythm of the words as I read them. That's not really right, but I can't explain it. It's just that some parts of the Quran seem to echo in the physical world. I don't know. It's weird."

"It's God," he said.

"I understand a little bit better where you're coming from now," I said. "Not just about God, but about … other things too. If everyone read this book, wow. Things would be different. The entire world would be different."

"And you will be different," he said. "When you declare your faith, all your sins will be forgiven. Everything you have ever done will be forgiven. You will start a new life. You will be a new person."

I didn't *tell* him I was changing my political beliefs to match his. I'm not sure he'd believe me if I did. And he'd be right not to believe me. If anything, my political beliefs were now further from his than they already were. But if the thought occurred to *him* that I might be changing my politics, he'd be more likely to believe it.

Even if I did intend to convert to Islam, I wouldn't necessarily change my views of anything else. Look at Stephen Schwartz. He's a slightly famous half-Jewish (on his father's side) writer and intellectual who was raised an atheist by radical leftist parents, but he became a Sufi Muslim in the Balkans, changed his name to Stephen Suleiman Schwartz, and registered as a Republican. It would never have even occurred to him to adopt Ahmed's politics just because he converted to Islam from atheism.

But he and Ahmed think differently. For Ahmed, and for all the world's Islamists, religion and politics are inseparable. They're a package. All I had to do was tell him I was moving closer to God. In his mind, it logically followed that I was moving closer to his "resistance" ideology too.

I had to be careful, though. He needed to think that each day brought me closer to Islam, but I could never get so close that it was time to convert. I recalled the Greek philosopher Zeno of Elea, whose series of mathematical paradoxes proved that if each day I covered half the remaining distance from secularism to Islam, I'd never actually get there. A tiny sliver of distance would forever remain no matter how close I got.

I could never let Ahmed pressure me into speaking the Shahada, the Islamic declaration of belief. *La ilaha il Allah, Muhammad-ur-Rasool-Allah.* There is no God but God and Muhammad is his messenger. Anyone who says these words in the presence of Muslim witnesses officially becomes a Muslim.

I may have been faking the process, but conversion during captivity sometimes happens.

Ever hear of British journalist Yvonne Ridley? In 2001 the Taliban kidnapped her in Afghanistan. She promised her captors she would read the Quran, and after returning home she converted to Islam. She dresses like a conservative Muslim woman now and wears a headscarf over her hair.

Not only did she change her religion, she changed her politics. She didn't just become a Muslim. She became an activist on behalf of Islamists. She took a job with Press TV, the international English-language propaganda channel for the Islamic Republic regime in Iran. Ismail Haniyah, the leader of Hamas in the Gaza Strip, rewarded her with a Palestinian passport. She was a champion of women's rights once but now slams the feminist critique of the veil and of women's rights in the Muslim world in general.

Maybe she still would have converted to Islam and championed reactionary Middle Eastern terrorists and regimes if the Taliban hadn't kidnapped her. Perhaps she suffered from such a debilitating case of Stockholm syndrome that it changed her forever. I don't know, and maybe she doesn't either.

Either way, Ahmed almost certainly knew all about her. Maybe he hoped from the very beginning that I'd transform myself in a similar way. He did say he thought everyone in the world was a potential convert to Islam. And why shouldn't he? It really is the world's fastest-growing religion. And he was a convert himself.

Not everyone who is kidnapped suffers from Stockholm syndrome. Women may be more susceptible to it than men. One theory posits it as a survival trait from our primitive hunter-gatherer days, when our female ancestors were frequently captured by hostile bands. Those who were able to bond with their captors and raise children with them spread their genes. Those who couldn't bond with their captors and raise children with them did not. So the capture-bonding trait was passed down. At least that's the theory.

I managed to resist it most of the time. But what if every one of my captors was like Ismail? (Or what if my captors were women?) What if there was no good-cop-bad-cop routine? What if all of them were good cops? I did feel myself more drawn to and trusting of Ismail than was healthy. I even felt that way about Ahmed to an extent when he was nice to me. I sincerely felt he had a decent side to him buried somewhere. Did he really, though? Or did I just choose to believe that because it made me feel safer?

What if they kept me prisoner for years and punished improper thoughts and behavior with pain and rewarded proper thoughts and behavior with pleasure? How long could I keep being me?

Ahmed shook me awake the next morning when the first light of dawn was beginning to break open the sky. I saw the dim shapes of him and Mahmoud standing over me. I gasped in alarm, but Ahmed said, "Shh."

"Come, brother," Mahmoud said softly. "Prayer is better than sleep."

That afternoon Ahmed finally let me out of the room and invited me to join him and the others.

"Brother," he said. "Sit next to me on the couch."

I sat and felt like a free man at last. Ahmed and Mahmoud both beamed at me. Ismail's face was positively radiant. Rat Bastard—Tariq—sat in a recliner across the room and wouldn't face me directly. He looked at me askance with a pinched mouth.

Give me a chance, I wanted to say. *I'm one of you now, and I won't let you down.*

"Getting to this point was hard for you, I know," Ahmed said. "I'm sorry about that. Really, I am. It was hard for me too. My parents hardly want to talk to me anymore. We fight every time I go to their house. They hate their religion. They hate where they come from."

Part of me—a far larger part than I'd like to admit—yearned to embrace Ahmed's religion with all my heart so he would accept me. I wanted him to like me. I wanted him to trust me. I wanted him to feel like I was his brother so that he'd let me live.

Another part of myself was screaming inside.

"So, listen," Ahmed said. "It's time to let you in on a couple of things. Eventually we'll want to get you back on the blogging, but we're going to have to ease into that slowly. Right now we have something more important for you to do. Think of it as an initiation."

I gulped.

"You must know we've been raising money," he said.

I exhaled, perhaps a little too loudly, because Rat Bastard noticed and narrowed his eyes at me. No one needed to be a psychic to read that look on his face. *What are you thinking?* he silently demanded. *What are you up to?*

"I've done some fundraising work in the past," I said, which was true.

"Not this kind, brother," Ahmed said and laughed. "Our operations cost millions of dollars."

Where did they get that kind of money? Al Qaeda was financed by the spectacularly wealthy Osama bin Laden, but he's dead now, buried at sea after SEAL Team Six whacked him in Pakistan. Hezbollah got its millions from the Iranian government and from massive drug operations in South America and Lebanon's Bekaa Valley. The Taliban got cash from opium farms in Afghanistan and from wealthy Gulf Arabs.

"So how do we get money?" I said. Ahmed's eyes lit up when I said the word *we*.

"The old-fashioned way," he said. "From banks."

I glanced over at Mahmoud, who stared at me with a deadly intensity. He patted his right boot with his hand. Did he keep a pistol down there under his pants leg?

"You rob banks," I said. It wasn't really a question.

Mahmoud nodded.

"We do," Ahmed said. "You're coming with us on the next run."

I swallowed hard and glanced around uneasily. What was I supposed to say? He didn't *ask* if I wanted to go with him.

"I don't know how to rob banks," I said.

"We do," Ahmed said. "We've done it several times."

My face felt flushed and my stomach twisted in knots. I was scared and they knew it. There was no hiding it now.

"You weren't caught?"

"Of course we weren't caught!" Ahmed said.

Of course they weren't caught. Otherwise they'd be in jail. I was babbling now and couldn't think clearly.

"I don't know how to rob a bank without getting caught," I said.

"You're not going to *do* anything," Ahmed said. "You're just coming with us."

"If I'm not going to do anything," I said, "then why do you want me to go with you?"

He just looked at me without saying anything. He was testing me. He was testing me to see how I'd respond. He'd be testing me at the bank too.

Or perhaps I had to go with them because they were behind on their quota. They had to hit another bank and they had to do it right then. And they couldn't leave me alone. I might yell for help. And this time, at the new location, someone might hear me. Maybe Ahmed was only pretending to trust me a little, only pretending to believe I was changing. What if everybody was bullshitting everybody? I had no idea what the fuck was going on.

I had to say the right thing, and fast.

"I suppose," I said, "that I'll learn how if I tag along with you the first time. And maybe I can participate in the next one."

Rat Bastard still wouldn't look at me. He wasn't buying any of it. He still wanted to shoot me and dump me in the forest. That much was obvious. If Ahmed trusted me, I'd be okay, but Ahmed still didn't trust me.

"We'll see how the first run goes," he said.

"I'll need a gun," I said.

Rat Bastard laughed.

"Tariq!" Ahmed said.

Rat Bastard pursed his lips and shook his head.

"You're not getting a gun," Ahmed said.

"But if we're robbing a bank—" I said.

"You're not getting a gun," Ahmed said again.

I remembered a story I heard in Iraq from a colleague of mine named Ramon, who worked for the Spanish newspaper *El País* in Madrid. He and I were embedded in the same U.S. Army unit in Baghdad. And he told me about the time Hamas kidnapped him in Gaza.

Hamas didn't intend to kill him or hold him for long. Ramon was never entirely sure why they grabbed him in the first place. Gaza at the time was a battleground between the Islamist militants of Hamas and secular Fatah forces with the Palestinian Authority. Various groups kidnapped Westerners once in a while and used them as pawns in their battle against others for control of the strip. The whole thing made no sense to casual observers of the Israeli-Palestinian conflict, and it hardly made any more sense to people like me and Ramon, who wrote about the Middle East for a living, but it happened, and Ramon spent four hours in captivity when Hamas thought he might be useful.

Young men wearing black ski masks grabbed him off the street, pulled a hood over his head, and bundled him off. When they finally took off the hood, he found himself in a room surrounded by a dozen or so men holding AK-47s.

"They were nice," he told me, "and they gave me tea, but I was very cross and they could see that. So one of them handed me his AK-47."

"Why on earth did he do that?" I said.

"To make me feel better," he said. Of course, there was no chance he could shoot his way out of that room, not with eleven other men holding similar rifles. They knew he would not even try. They planned to let him go anyway as soon a deal was struck with the Palestinian Authority, so there was no harm in letting him hold onto a weapon. And he said it *did* make him feel better.

I wanted to tell Ahmed that story but thought better of it. I was a kidnapping victim just like Ramon was, but I needed Ahmed to think we were moving beyond that and forging a new kind of relationship, the kind Yvonne Ridley had with her captors.

But Ahmed still didn't trust me.

"Don't you think," I said, "that I'll be less effective if I don't have a gun? What if someone in the bank tries to overpower me?"

"We can't give you a gun right now, Michael," Ahmed said.

"What are you worried I'll do?" I said. "Shoot all *four* of you in the bank lobby and run?"

"It's not that we don't trust you," he said.

"I don't trust him," Rat Bastard said.

"Tariq," Ahmed snapped. "I'll handle this."

He turned then to me.

"I trust you," he said. "Mostly. Tariq isn't certain."

Rat Bastard snorted.

"We're all moving at different speeds here," Ahmed said. "I'm certain you still have trust issues yourself. You have every right to have trust issues yourself. Especially when it comes to Tariq." He shot Rat Bastard an angry look. Rat Bastard lowered his gaze.

"Give me a gun without any ammo then," I said.

Ahmed stuck out his jaw and nodded slightly. "You're right that you'll be less effective if you don't have a gun. So we'll give you one without any cartridges. And of course you'll wear a ski mask like the rest of us. We can't let anyone see our faces, and especially not yours, since you've been on TV."

Mahmoud nodded solemnly at me.

"And, by the way," Ahmed said as matter-of-factly as if we were talking about breakfast. "If I turn out to be wrong about you, if you try to run or take off your mask, Mahmoud will—you know. And he'll do it slowly enough that you'll die from a heart attack."

This time Mahmoud just stared.

"You can go back to your room now," Ahmed said.

So Ahmed didn't want me to be the next Yvonne Ridley. He wanted me to be the next Patty Hearst, the granddaughter of famous newspaper tycoon William Randolph Hearst. She was kidnapped by the so-called Symbionese Liberation Army in 1974 when she was just nineteen years old.

The SLA were leftists opposed to the Vietnam War and "the establishment," and they declared war on the United States government. They robbed banks to get money to fund operations. Presumably, they kidnapped Hearst because she was famous, or at least her grandfather was, and so they could use her to get boatloads of media attention. It worked too. Her story, and theirs, made its way into every newspaper and onto every news channel in America.

The most extraordinary twist came when she announced on the radio that she had joined the SLA after two months in captivity. She later claimed they'd locked her in a closet and brainwashed her—Maoist style—but in the meantime she joined them in a spree of bank robberies and in 1976 was sentenced to seven years in prison. President Jimmy Carter, convinced that she'd been manipulated, pardoned her in 1979.

But I was no Patty Hearst. There had to be something I could do to escape or alert the police once we got to the bank. I couldn't shoot my way free. I wouldn't be able to shoot my way free even if I had ammunition.

And I couldn't even get ammunition. I didn't know where Ahmed kept it and I certainly couldn't go poking around. I couldn't even walk around loose in the house.

Ahmed had said I could go back to my room. He didn't say I *had* to go back to my room. Technically, all he did was give me permission. No one bolted me in after I shut the door, but I knew I was expected to stay there and keep quiet. And I complied.

That's when I realized I was changing. I was building invisible chains for myself. I stayed in my room even though the door wasn't locked and nobody said I had to.

Ahmed and the rest of the gang couldn't keep me prisoner indefinitely unless one of two things happened. Either they'd chain me to a radiator, Hezbollah-style, or my own mind would create invisible walls that I wouldn't let myself pass through.

It happens to kidnapping victims a lot, especially children. I've lost track of how many times I've read about kids being taken by strangers and held for many years, who were eventually allowed out of their captor's house to run to the store to get milk. The kids would return from the store on their own! They could run away and get help, but instead they'd return on their own.

Adult kidnapping victims rarely reach that stage of surrender, but the same parts of our minds that allow us to become so completely imprisoned as children are still active as we grow older. I never quite understood how any of this was possible until Ahmed left me in an unlocked room and I did not try to leave. They had kept me prisoner long enough by then that I had completely internalized the fact that they had control.

At least I had almost completely internalized it. Part of my mind knew what was happening. They didn't actually have total control. If I was aware of the fact that I was creating invisible walls for myself, I wouldn't forget that those walls were not real. I'd remember that I could, in fact, make a break for it. But I'd have to choose my moment carefully. If I tried and failed to flee even once after pretending to be converting to Islam, they'd kill me. When it went down, I'd have one shot and one shot only.

I didn't yet know what to do, but I knew I had to do something. I couldn't just go with them while they robbed a bank and obey like a good boy. If I had access to pen and paper, I could write a small note, crumple it up into a ball, and drop it on the floor when no one was looking. The police would scour the crime scene for every last trace of evidence. That's what they do. They'd look for something as small as an eyelash. If I left a note, surely they'd find it even if it was written on a discarded gum wrapper. But how could I leave a note? I didn't even have a matchbook to write on.

So once again, I pretended I was writing a novel. What would I have my character do if I was sitting at my desk and making everything up? My character, the fictional version of Michael J. Totten, would have to leave some kind of message for the police. That much I knew. But the first thing I'd have to do as an author is figure out what that message would be.

The police would need to know who we were. They'd need to know that I'm Michael J. Totten. Ahmed said my face was all over the TV and in all the papers, so every news junkie in the country must have known who I was. If the local cops didn't know, they'd find out as soon as they punched my name into their database at the station.

The police would also need to know where Ahmed and the others were keeping me, but even I didn't know. I wasn't even sure which state we were in. If I'd had to guess, I would have said Idaho, but that would have been a guess. I imagined myself in a mountainous forest north of Boise, but we could have been near Missoula or Portland, for all I really knew. So I couldn't tell the police where the cabin was located. I could, however, tell the police we were in an isolated vacation cabin. How many could there be in a particular area? A few dozen? A hundred at most? Surely the police would rule out several that we couldn't be in. We weren't in a crowded area at a ski resort, for instance. There were no neighbors around, at least none I could see.

All I had to do was give the police a couple of leads. Even one or two leads might be enough for them to figure it out and come get me.

Part of me was reluctant, however. The last time I tried to signal for help, two people were shot. And all I had done was mouth of a couple of words with a harried look on my face.

Then it hit me. I could do the same thing again, only this time I could mouth the words to a security camera. A security camera wouldn't react and give me away. All I had to do was locate one in the corner near the ceiling and silently mouth the words *Michael Totten, kidnapped,* and *vacation cabin.* The police would surely review the tapes and figure it out. And this time, no one would have any idea what I was doing. So that was it, then. That was the plan.

I heard a knock on my door.

"Yes?" I said.

"Get some sleep." It was Ahmed. "We're going first thing in the morning."

Chapter Eleven

I could barely sleep all night and was already wide awake when Ahmed knocked on my door.

"You up?" he said. "We leave in an hour."

"Yeah, I'm up, thanks," I said.

Our relationship really was changing. He never knocked in the first house. He barged in whenever he wanted. But now he was acting like a courteous housemate.

I assumed that the shared experience of a stressful event like a bank robbery would make us feel even closer. It happens to soldiers in war. It happens to a lesser degree to hikers who take long backpacking trips together and have to rely on each other to survive in the wilderness. Perhaps that was why Ahmed wanted me to go with them. He figured it might help me bond with them. But if they felt it too, I could turn it around and convince them to trust me, and to trust me more than they should.

"Come on out when you're ready," Ahmed said.

I brushed my teeth, splashed water on my face, and put on some clothes. I hardly recognized myself in the mirror. I hadn't shaved in two weeks. If I put sunglasses on, my own wife might not even recognize me. Even without sunglasses, my eyes sagged as though I had aged years.

I could hear them loading their weapons on the other side of the door. Even if you've never been around real guns in your life, the sound a magazine makes as it's slammed home is unmistakable. I also heard one of them loading shotgun shells and had to wonder: Why on earth would anyone bring a shotgun to a bank robbery? It would be much harder to conceal on the way in and out.

When I opened the door to the living room, I froze. All four wore black ski masks and turned at the same time to look at me. All four had guns in their hands. Mahmoud held the shotgun. He had sawed off the barrel. They were ready for terrorism and war.

And their ski masks covered their entire faces, including their mouths, leaving just slits for eyes.

"Here," Ahmed said and handed me one. "Put this on."

I stretched it out and, sure enough, the one they wanted me to wear would cover my mouth, as well. How was I supposed to silently speak to a security camera while wearing a mask that covered my mouth? A sour taste rose from the back of my throat, and my legs went weak at the knees.

"You okay?" Ahmed said.

"He's afraid," Rat Bastard said.

"Yeah," I said. "To be honest, I am." I swallowed. "This is pretty intense."

Ahmed nodded. I'd have a hard time telling them apart if none of them said anything. Only Mahmoud was obvious with his girth.

"You'll be fine," Ahmed said. "Here." He handed me a pistol, a lightweight Glock 17, the model with the rubber-wrap grip. "There's one round in the chamber in case you need it."

I must have looked as dumbstruck as I felt.

"Go ahead," he said. "Check."

I opened the chamber and, yep, there was a cartridge in there. I imagined myself raising the pistol and shooting Ahmed in the face.

If they *really* wanted to test my loyalty, they should have handed me a gun loaded with blanks and then set their weapons down.

That had to be a real cartridge in the chamber. They knew there was a chance that things could get ugly for us.

"I need to give you one more thing," Ahmed said. "And for this one I apologize."

"What?" I said. He wasn't carrying anything else.

"Mahmoud," he said.

Mahmoud pulled a black bandanna out of his pocket.

"We need to blindfold you in the car on the way over," Ahmed said.

"Come on, guys," I said.

"I'm sorry," Ahmed said, "but we have to. Think about this from our point of view."

Of course, I understood. He didn't want me to know where the cabin was located, nor did he want me to see anything beyond our immediate surroundings. Perhaps there was another cabin just a hundred or so yards away. Maybe there was even a *town* just down the road. I couldn't hear any cars, but the forest would muffle the sounds of traffic even if the nearest road was only a half-mile away. A fit person can run a half-mile in a panicked sprint in, what, two or three minutes?

Ahmed couldn't allow me to plan an escape once I saw the route out. Nor could he give me information about our location that I could pass on at the bank. But how was I supposed to send a message at the bank when I had nothing to write with and I'd have my entire face covered? I didn't know sign language or Morse code.

But when I stuck the gun down the front of my pants, I felt a thrilling rush of control for the first time since they took me. The ground had shifted. Something had changed that would not be undone by the blindfold Mahmoud was about to place over my eyes. If I kept playing my role and playing it perfectly, they'd give me incrementally more and more freedom until the inevitable time would come when they'd make a mistake.

First, though, we had a bank to rob. Mahmoud gently placed the blindfold over my eyes.

So there I was, riding blind in the van again. I was used to it by now, and at least this time I didn't worry that they were going to shoot me. But I was on my way to a bank robbery with a loaded gun in my hand.

A friend of mine who used to work at a bank became morbidly fascinated with robberies. He researched them on the Internet and found that an enormous percentage of bank robbers are shot by the police instead of arrested. Partly it's because the police pursue bank robbers with zeal, but mostly it's because people who rob banks are the types who refuse to go quietly. The cops know this better than anyone. They always show up with their weapons drawn and ready for kill shots.

As we pulled away from the cabin on a gravel road, I paid as much attention as possible to what I could hear and what I could feel. I couldn't see anything with the blindfold on, but I constructed a hazy mental image of our route.

Gravel crunched under our tires as the road gently curved a bit to the left and the right. Then we took a hard right turn onto a paved road and picked up speed. I didn't hear any oncoming cars, but I couldn't be sure that there weren't any behind or in front of us going the same direction. Either way, the road wasn't busy. That much was clear. Wherever we were, it was still a remote area.

After a minute or two, though, we had to stop for a bit (presumably at a stop sign) and wait for traffic to clear before making a left. I imagined black pavement with a yellow stripe down the middle and wide shoulders on each side with a dense forest of fir trees framing the scene. Perhaps there were some large green road signs with reflective white letters counting down the miles to our destination. But what was our destination?

I kept bouncing my knees and pulling at my pant legs. I couldn't sit still, couldn't stay comfortable.

"We don't use our real names inside," Ahmed said as we drove. "Michael, your code name is Zack. Your name isn't Michael Totten anymore. It's Zack Thomas. If any of us need to get your attention, we're calling you Zack. Internalize that. Imagine turning your head when you hear me say *Zack*."

"Got it," I said. I felt like one of them at that moment. And the pistol felt good in my hand.

"My name on the inside is *Andy*," he said. "Mahmoud's is *Mark*. Ismail's is *Ivan*. And Tariq's is *Tom*. You should be able to keep all that straight because our real names and our code names start with the same letter. Except for yours."

"Okay," I said. "Andy. Mark. Ivan. And Tom."

I wondered if Ahmed was really his name or if that was a code name, as well. Maybe his real name was Mohamed. Andy was most likely a code name for a code name.

After a half-hour or so, we slowed into traffic and had to stop at red lights. We were in a city, not a small town, but I had no idea which. It could have been Boise, Spokane, or Pendleton. Possibly even Portland.

I assumed we were in Boise, but that was a guess. I had to be careful not to assume it too strongly in case I was wrong, but I couldn't create a mental map in my head without filling in some details that were bound to be off.

"There it is," Rat Bastard said. "Just up ahead."

"Lock and load," Ismail said, and I cringed inside. Was it really Ismail who said that? Or was it Rat Bastard? I was blind, but I wasn't deaf and I could swear it was Ismail. What kind of man was he, really?

The van pulled off the main street and into a parking lot. I figured the bank had to be in the suburbs. Downtowns usually require street parking. We had driven for forty-five minutes, an hour at most. That cabin had to be somewhere within a sixty-mile radius.

Mahmoud pumped his shotgun. *Here we go.*

"Everyone ready?" Ahmed said.

A meaty hand pulled the blindfold off my eyes, and I squinted at the blazing sunshine coming in through the windshield.

"Just a second," I said. "My eyes need to adjust."

I wanted to look around, but the van had no side windows. All I could see through the windshield was a brick wall, presumably the side of the bank. Once that van door opened, I'd only have a few seconds to look around and figure out where we were before going in.

Ahmed sat in the passenger seat. He wasn't yet wearing his mask, though the others were. Tariq—Rat Bastard—was in the driver's seat, but he had his head between his knees so no one could see him. We couldn't let anyone see a van full of guys wearing ski masks in the parking lot of a bank. Ismail and Mahmoud were in the back with me, masked up and ready to go.

Ahmed scanned the parking lot with his hand over his face as if he were shielding his eyes from the sun. If there were any security cameras mounted on the exterior walls—and there probably were—they wouldn't get a good look at him. I assumed they'd put stolen license plates from another state on the van. They must have had a whole set of them.

"Hold still," Ahmed said. "A man and a woman are coming out. I don't see anyone else, but let's wait for them to get in their car and pull into the street."

I could hear the man and woman talking to each other, but I couldn't quite make out what they were saying. Whatever they were talking about was enviably mundane. They were they talking about dinner, perhaps, or about who was going to take the kids to band practice. Maybe they were wondering aloud if they should take their next vacation in Europe or the Caribbean. God, what I would have given at the moment to have a normal conversation like that with my wife. Their timing was impeccable. If they hadn't emerged from the lobby right when they did, they would have found themselves with Mahmoud's sawed-off in their faces.

I heard them get into a vehicle and close the doors, followed by the sound of the engine turning over.

"Another car just pulled into the lot," Ahmed said. He leaned forward and dug around in the glove box, trying to look normal while keeping his face out of sight.

"*Man*," Rat Bastard said and blew out his breath. He sounded as stressed out as I was. How long were we going to sit there?

"We'll follow them in," Ahmed said, "as long as it's otherwise clear."

I took a deep breath.

"Michael," Ahmed said. "Zack. You're Zack now, remember? Stay next to me. And don't say anything to *anyone* unless you have to."

Mahmoud whispered a brief prayer in Arabic.

I looked at the gun in my hand, still amazed that they let me have one. They were smart to give me only one round, but what was to stop me from shooting Mahmoud the minute we stepped out of the van, taking his gun, and finishing the rest of them off? Truthfully, I wasn't brave enough. I'd rather make myself an accessory to bank robbery and remain under their control. I hated myself for it but vowed to fight my way free in the future if my odds looked even a little bit better. Maybe this experience at the bank would make them trust me just enough that they'd make a fatal mistake.

They might even make a fatal mistake in the bank. I *did* have one round. And I was prepared to use it if the precisely right moment presented itself. If the cops come storming in, I could take Mahmoud out and likely survive as long as I timed my shot perfectly, but I'd need to make sure the cops don't see me shoot Mahmoud or they might shoot me.

I took another deep breath. So did Rat Bastard. Mahmoud cracked his neck from side to side and rolled his shoulders forward and back.

"We run into that bank as fast as we can," Ahmed said. "*No one* can see us in this parking lot. Got it?"

I had an idea. What if I let all of them run in ahead of me? What if they run in the bank while I turn and run into the street?

"Zack," Ahmed said and leaned forward. "You're going first." I felt myself deflate like a balloon that just came untied. "I'll be right behind you."

He still didn't trust me. Oh, how I wished I knew why he brought me along. Was he testing me? Training me? Babysitting me? Trying to create a bonding experience? *What?*

"Okay," Ahmed said and pulled the mask over his head. "They're in. Go!"

Mahmoud slammed the door open. I felt like I was standing at the open hatch of a plane getting ready to jump out at 10,000 feet without a parachute. Ismail shoved me in the back. He wasn't the man I wanted him to be.

"Go!" Ahmed yelled. "Zack!"

I ran toward the double-glass doors, hoping to take in as much information about my surroundings as possible, but there was nothing to see aside from a few parked cars, a two-lane road alongside the building, and a Jiffy Lube across the street. As I pushed one of the swinging doors open, I saw the words "Boise First Savings and Loan" stenciled onto the glass. I was right. We were in Boise! Or at least we were in Idaho. Or at least we were robbing a bank that had its headquarters in Idaho.

As the five of us poured into the lobby, the energy of my captors was like nothing I'd seen. They were deadly serious, hopped up on masculinity and adrenaline, and they moved in perfectly terrifying military formation.

Just short of a dozen people waited in line for one of the tellers.

Mahmoud pumped his shotgun, a tactically pointless action since it was already loaded, but it sure had an effect. A woman in a tan business coat screamed. A middle-aged man standing next to her yelled "Shit!" and hit the floor. Another man at a desk gasped and ducked his head behind a computer monitor. Everyone else just flinched and then froze. They knew at once why we were there.

"If anyone hits an alarm," Ahmed said and waved his gun around the room, "we're taking *all* of you hostage!"

A young female bank teller put her hand on her mouth and gaped at him in raw terror.

"If the cops get here before we leave," Ahmed said, "you could be stuck with us in here for *days*. Cooperate and we'll be gone in less than five minutes."

"Everybody down on the ground!" Rat Bastard said.

Everyone dropped, including the teller. The woman in the tan coat grabbed hold of a balding man lying next to her and would not let him go. Ahmed ran up to the teller's window.

"You!" he said. "Get back up here."

She stood and raised her shaking hands in the air.

I scanned the room for security cameras and found one behind me over the doors we walked through. There were two more on the wall above the tellers that filmed and photographed everybody in line and at the counter. I desperately wanted to rip off my mask for those cameras, or at least lift it enough so that whoever played back the tape could see my mouth and lip-read a message. But I knew if I did that, Ahmed would agree with Rat Bastard that it was finally time to put me down in the forest, if not right there on the bank floor.

I stood next to Ahmed at the teller's window. She looked at me with more sheer fright on her face than I'd ever seen on a person, her eyes like those of a panicked animal that just caught sight of a charging, flesh-ripping predator.

Ahmed handed her a potato sack. "Fill it," he said. "If you put anything in there besides money, I'll shoot your guts out."

I believed him. She did too. If someone ever threatens to kill you and isn't bluffing, *you'll know.*

She stuffed money into the bag. Lots of it.

"You!" Rat Bastard said to someone behind me, presumably the man at one of the desks. "Open the vault!"

"Okay," the man said between hyperventilations. "Okay, okay."

I turned around and saw him emerge from behind a desk with his hands over his head. He shook his fingers in the air, as if he could make everything go away if he could only wave hard enough.

A woman in a floral-print dress lay shuddering on her stomach at my feet. A man lying next to her had wet himself. I could see a puddle of urine spreading toward his knees. A small boy I hadn't even noticed when we came in cried and buried his face into his mother's back.

My heart pounded in my chest, and my breath burst in and out. I grabbed onto the counter for balance. These people had no idea, but I was just as frightened as they were, if not even more so. At least none of them would have to leave the bank and go *with* these men.

I watched as the man from behind the desk passed through a small gate in the counter and walked toward the vault. And just on the periphery of my vision, I noticed another man rise from the floor in the back of the lobby. I turned and looked. He held a pistol in his hand and raised it toward Ismail.

"Gun!" I yelled instinctively. "Watch out!"

I could have shot him. I had one round in the chamber of my own weapon. But there was no chance I'd do that, not to save one of my captors. Not even to save Ismail. But what if the man aimed at me?

Ismail and Rat Bastard frantically turned to see who had just drawn a weapon, but it was too late. The man aimed right at the side of Ismail's center of mass and fired a bullet straight into his rib cage. Ismail went down hard on his ass with his legs splayed out in front of him, a rose of blood blossoming under his armpit.

That was when everything changed. Time slowed. I heard Ahmed yell "No!" but it sounded like his voice was playing at half-speed. Screams. I couldn't tell if their voices were male or female. Mahmoud turned his head slowly. At least it appeared to me that he turned his head slowly. He saw a shocked and bloodied Ismail on the floor. Rat Bastard turned in alarm. Turned in alarm toward the man with the gun. The man with the gun was up on his knees now. He raised his pistol again. Pointed it directly at Ahmed.

Rat Bastard pulled the trigger and shot the man just below the heart.

Time sped back up.

Mahmoud yelled something in Arabic. I could not make it out, but everyone heard him.

"They aren't bank robbers!" yelled the woman in the tan coat on the floor. "They're terrorists!"

There was something absurd about her assuming we were terrorists just because Mahmoud said a few words in Arabic, but she was right. Mahmoud bared his teeth, tensed up his arms and his neck, and blew her head apart with his shotgun. Sounded like an exploding car bomb. Time slowed again to almost a stop. Blood, gore, and brain matter splattered in every direction. Ahmed leaned over the counter and retched.

Mahmoud pumped his shotgun. An empty shell slowly tumbled in the air and clattered onto the floor. A man next to the dead woman rolled away from her slowly. Even Rat Bastard looked at Mahmoud with shock and alarm. And Mahmoud pulled the trigger again, this time blowing apart the abdomen of another woman on the floor.

"My God," Ahmed said. "'Mood, no."

I could have aimed at Mahmoud and pulled the trigger, but my hands were shaking so badly, I would almost certainly miss. I had only one round. So I lunged at him, hoping to knock him over so someone could get that gun out of his hands.

And then somebody shot me.

Chapter Twelve

I drifted in an ethereal fog and faintly heard screams, explosions of gunfire, and the smacking of arms, legs, and hands on marble flooring. Everything sounded like it was happening underwater. Tendrils of pain shot from my right shoulder through my entire body, all the way down to the bottom of my feet, but I didn't mind. I was aware of the pain but somehow unbothered by it.

My breathing was labored, however. Something covered my face, a cloth of some kind. No, it was a ski mask. I reached up and pulled it off so I could breathe.

I heard a voice I vaguely knew belonged to someone named Ahmed say, "Is he dead?" Was who dead? Me? I wasn't dead. At least I didn't think so. I just wanted to sleep.

"He's gone," someone else said. Someone named Tariq, I think. Oh. It was Rat Bastard.

Wait a minute.

I was on my back looking up at the ceiling and I heard a booming car bomb. Or was it a shotgun?

Shit. Mahmoud was shooting people.

Screams of dying agony.

"Make him stop," somebody said. I think it was Rat Bastard.

I tried to sit up but couldn't. I was paralyzed. And cold. My mouth was dry. Part of me dimly understood that I was in shock.

My eyes worked, but I couldn't see what was happening, not lying on my back. All I could see was the ceiling, the sprinkler system, flickering fluorescent lights overhead, and a camera mounted high on the wall.

A security camera! I remembered what I needed to do. I had

rehearsed it in my mind dozens of times. My mask was off and nobody seemed to be paying the slightest bit of attention to me.

"Michael Totten," I said in a voice too faint for anybody to hear. "Kidnapped."

Another explosive blast from Mahmoud's shotgun.

"Terrorists," I said. "Vacation cabin. One hour away."

It was all I could do, though I was pretty sure it was all I needed to do. I managed to roll my head a bit to the side and saw the gun Ahmed had given me lying just beyond reach. I had a round in the chamber, but I couldn't quite grab it.

I closed my eyes and tried to will myself into sleep and felt several sets of hands lift me up off the floor. My left shoulder exploded in agony. This time it hurt like a motherfucker and everything faded to black.

I felt like every bone in my upper body was shattered and that a railroad spike had been hammered into my shoulder. That agonizing pain was the only thing that existed. I felt it long and hard before I woke up and opened my eyes. When I did open my eyes and let out a whimper, I saw Rat Bastard—Tariq—looking down at me.

"He's awake," he said.

Was I in a hospital? No. We were back at the cabin. They had placed me on the bed in my room. I reached a hand toward my shoulder, but Rat Bastard stopped me with his own.

"Don't touch it," he said softly. "Or it will start bleeding again."

Ahmed stepped into view. "How are you feeling?" he said with genuine concern in his voice. He wasn't faking it. I could see it in his eyes. He was worried about me.

"It hurts," I said and groaned. I lifted my head off the pillow a bit so I could see the damage for myself. They'd plugged my shoulder with toilet paper and secured it with duct tape. Guys like them should have had quick clot. It's available at outdoor stores. I loudly exhaled as I set my head down again. "I need to get to a hospital," I said.

"You know we can't take you to a hospital," Ahmed said. "But it's okay. You aren't going to die from it." He reached into his pocket and pulled out a little white bottle. "Here," he said, stepping forward and handing it to me. "It's ibuprofen. Take twelve. Tariq, get him some water."

Tariq left the room and headed for the kitchen.

"Ibuprofen won't do shit for a gunshot wound," I said. "That's what this is, right? I've been shot?"

"You've been shot," Ahmed said and nodded.

I heard Tariq open the tap in the sink. He was letting the water run cold before filling my glass.

"You didn't shoot me," I said.

"No," Ahmed said and chuckled. "It was—that man. He shot you after Tariq shot him. Mahmoud took care of it."

Then I remembered. It all came back in a flood. Mahmoud committed a massacre in that bank.

I felt hot and couldn't swallow. I tried to sit up, but the pain in my shoulder turned into a supernova.

"Easy," Ahmed said.

Tariq returned with a tall glass of water. Ahmed held the back of my head so I could drink. I only intended to sip from the glass, but the water was deliciously cold, and the minute I took the first swallow I realized I was severely dehydrated. I finished the entire glass before taking any pills.

"Can I have some more, please?" I said.

"Of course," Tariq said.

He no longer seemed like a rat bastard now that he was talking to me like a regular human being and bringing me water.

"Ismail?" I said.

"Dead," Ahmed said. His eyes were unfocused, and a blank expression washed over his face.

I sighed. I was sorry as hell to hear that. Really, I was. I never wished destruction on Ismail. Of the four, he was the one I thought might be able to reform himself someday. Few human beings are evil all the way through, and hardly anyone perceives himself to be evil, but of the four, Ismail's decency and goodness were the easiest to see by far.

"Mahmoud—" I said.

Ahmed and Tariq looked at each other.

"He's outside," Ahmed said.

Silence.

"He's sitting on a stump out there and won't talk to either of us," Tariq said.

"That was brave, what you did," Ahmed said.

Brave? Me? What was he talking about? What did I do?

"I don't really remember what happened," I said, though I was lying. Or at least I thought I was lying. I remembered mouthing information to the security camera. Did I also do something I couldn't remember?

"You took a bullet for Mahmoud," Tariq said.

I did?

No, I did not. I knew exactly what happened. I lunged for Mahmoud after he shot a woman. I had no idea I was stepping into the path of an oncoming bullet. I thought Tariq had killed the man who was shooting at us, but he was apparently still alive. He was aiming at Mahmoud? *That* I didn't know. It hadn't occurred to me that I took a bullet for Mahmoud. I certainly hadn't done it on purpose.

"Everything happened so fast," I said.

So that's why Tariq was being nice all of a sudden. He finally trusted me. I had them exactly where I wanted them. They were bound to make a big mistake now. Only problem was that I had been shot. I couldn't even sit up, let alone run away.

I believed Ahmed when he said my shoulder wound wasn't fatal, but it felt like it was going to kill me. They say kidney stones are the most painful thing a person can live through, but it isn't true. I've had kidney stones twice. I got one in Iraq and one in Israel. I would *much* rather have a third kidney stone than get shot again.

"I'll take those Advils now," I said and winced.

Ahmed unscrewed the cap and poured a small handful of little orange pills into my palm. He held the back of my head again while I sipped from my refilled glass of water and swallowed.

"Can you guys get me some prescription meds?" I said. "One of you could tell a doctor you have a migraine or that you passed a kidney stone or whatever."

"It's too risky," Ahmed said. "I'm sorry. The police know you've been shot. Well, they don't know who has been shot, but they know one of us has been shot, and they'll be looking for us at all the hospitals and clinics for five hundred miles."

I wanted to say, *So drive me six hundred miles,* but I didn't.

I gasped. The pain was extraordinary. I wasn't hyperventilating exactly, but close. I tried to tell myself it wasn't pain I was feeling, just a hell of a strong sensation, but that didn't help.

"So what now?" I said and scrunched up my face.

"We're going to wait a few days," Ahmed said. "And then we're taking a boat."

Please, I thought. *Tell me we're taking a boat to Vancouver Island in Canada so I can get to a hospital.*

"Where?" I said.

"Algeria," he said.

I coughed and winced again from the pain.

"It's not as dangerous as it used to be," he said. "And, besides, you'll be under our protection."

I tried to sit up again, but Ahmed gently placed his hand on my chest.

"You need to rest," he said. "We're taking a boat, but it won't be ready for three days. We're setting off from the Puget Sound just north of Seattle. One of the men who will be joining us is a doctor. He'll fix your shoulder. You'll be mostly healed by the time we get to Algiers. You'll be comfortable. We can finish your religious conversion at sea. When you feel up for it."

"I need to talk to my wife," I said.

"That's impossible now," he said.

I could not let him see me cry.

"It's hard," he said. "I know. I'm so sorry this has happened to you, but look, we have a camp in the desert. It is so beautiful, Michael. You're going to love it. It's hot during the summer, but winter is coming, and it will cool off. We're stopping in Panama on the way for supplies before we go through the canal. You can call your wife from a town there, I promise. Just don't tell her where you are or where we're going. She will be so happy to hear from you."

The police should have had all the information they needed to solve the bank robbery. I remembered exactly what I had said into that security camera. *Michael Totten. Kidnapped. Terrorists. Vacation cabin. One hour away.* Surely they'd look at the tape. With a little digital enhancing, someone should be able read my lips and understand what I was saying. Right? As long as the film quality was decent enough. As long as Ahmed didn't find and pull the tape before we left. I was blacked out at that point and couldn't be sure. I had no idea if the fancy digital enhancing we see in cop shows is real. It probably isn't. But if those tapes couldn't make out many details, what were they for?

All the police had to do was canvass everyone who owned vacation cabins for rent within an hour's drive of the bank and show them pictures of Ismail. As long as he wasn't shot in the face, they'd have usable photographs. The case couldn't be that hard to solve. And the police should have been keenly motivated since Mahmoud killed so many people. As far as I knew, he killed *everyone*.

"Our support role," Ahmed said, "requires us to go to Algeria once in a while. We have all this cash to deliver. We can't deposit it and send it by wire transfer, not without the government finding out. So we deliver it to the base in Algeria in person. We were planning a trip there next month. We were going to hit one more bank before shoving off, but we're speeding things up now after … what happened."

"What *did* happen in there?" I said. "Mahmoud."

"Yeah," Ahmed said and looked at his feet.

"How many people did he kill?"

"I'm not sure," Ahmed said. "But he shot everyone."

"We couldn't stop him," Tariq said. "He just flew into a rage and wouldn't come out of it."

My God.

"But it was the right decision," Ahmed said. "We couldn't have any witnesses telling the police they heard one of us speaking Arabic. It was Mahmoud's fault, though, for speaking Arabic in the first place. He screwed up. He cleaned up his mess, but he screwed up. He won't be working with us anymore after we get to Algeria."

"He'll be moving into combat operations," Tariq said. "That's where he belongs. Not with us."

"Tariq will be going into combat operations, as well," Ahmed said. Tariq grinned. "We have a training camp there. I'll be the leader of a new support group. You can work with me. You'll finally learn fluent Arabic and can help us with messaging. You'll be perfect for that with all your journalism and writing experience."

"I need to get some more sleep," I said, but what I really needed was for them to get out of my room. There was no way I'd go with them to Algeria. If I had to wait until Panama to get away, then so be it. If I had to jump off a boat into the canal, then so be it. If I had to risk getting shot again, then so be it. I was not going with them to Algeria.

"We'll leave you alone," Ahmed said. "Your wife can join us when we get there. If she wants to. And don't worry. We won't expect her to convert right away. There's no compulsion in religion."

PART THREE

MARTYR'S DAY

Chapter Thirteen

They came at dawn while most of us slept. Mahmoud saw them. He was on watch, and he alerted us with a rifle shot into the trees when he spotted movement. A scout. Or maybe a sniper.

"Cops!" Tariq yelled from somewhere deep in the house. I felt a powerful surge of elation. *Rescued.* At last! Oh, how I wish I could have seen the look on Tariq's face.

The police must have planned a stealthy raid at first light when they hoped we were all still asleep, but the gunshot put an end to all that. So they switched to Plan B—shock and awe. I heard an avalanche of tires crunching on the gravel outside. There must have been twenty vehicles charging down the road.

I saw their red and blue lights flashing on the walls of my room, but I did not hear any sirens. One squad car after another skidded to a halt in the gravel outside, followed by a cascade of opening and slamming car doors.

Bare feet padded across the wood floor in the living room. Curtains slid open. Curtains slid closed.

The door to my bedroom burst open. Ahmed stood panting. "Police!" he said, his voice choked with emotion and his arms curled over his head. He looked wild.

"We're fucked," I said, knowing that was just what he wanted to hear, though most likely without the profanity. Did he still think I was one of them? Would he use me as a human shield? Would Mahmoud barge into the room and finish me off before I could be saved?

One of the officers shouted into a bullhorn. "Drop your weapons and come out with your hands up!"

Ahmed, panicked and trembling, turned toward the front door.

"'Mood!" he yelled.

Mahmoud answered in Arabic and rushed up to Ahmed with the sawed-off in his hand. They looked at each other and nodded.

Mahmoud glanced at me and huffed a deep breath. His facial expression was easy to read. *You're useless*, he thought as he saw me all shot and bandaged up on the bed. *A liability, actually.*

He hit the floor and crawled toward the front window on his belly with the shotgun gripped in both hands. He exuded perfect focus and calm. Tariq ducked behind the side of the couch armed with a pistol. Ahmed crouched in my doorway.

"We have you surrounded!" the officer outside yelled into the bullhorn. "Come out with your hands up and no one gets hurt!"

"*Allahu Akbar*," Tariq said. *God is great.* He half stood up from behind the side of the couch and slunk toward the window, keeping his head just barely below the windowsill.

Ahmed took Tariq's place beside the couch.

"What do we do?" Tariq said. "We fight?"

"I don't have a gun," Ahmed said.

Tariq had a second pistol tucked into the back of his pants. He fished it out and slid it across the wood floor. Ahmed picked it up and gripped it with both hands.

"We have you surrounded!" the policeman outside said again. "The only way you can come out is with your hands over your head!"

"Ready?" Tariq said. He was panting and sweating already.

"On three," Ahmed said.

These idiots were actually going to shoot at the cops. I had to get off the bed if bullets were going to fly. But my shoulder! The bullet was still lodged deep inside. I braced myself for the floor's impact and for the shooting pain of a lifetime.

"One," Ahmed said.

I rolled onto my right side. Pain erupted from my left shoulder like gushing lava and surged though my fingertips.

"Two," Ahmed said.

Jesus, they were really going to do it. I scooted myself to the edge of the bed, this time knowing how much it would hurt before I moved. It helps if you know in advance how much something is going to hurt.

"Three," Ahmed said.

I held my breath as I slid off the bed and screamed when I hit the floorboards. Gunshots shattered glass. Tariq's and Ahmed's pistols popped. Incoming rounds snapped into the walls. I looked toward the bathroom. I should get into the tub. I couldn't ward off the terrifying noise, but I could at least protect myself from bullets, splinters, and shards.

My left arm was useless, but I pulled myself across the floor with my right as Ahmed and Tariq fired out the window. I looked through my doorway and into the living room. Mahmoud lay on the floor beneath the main window. Ahmed crouched beneath the side window and pointed his pistol outside, shooting blindly.

Tariq bent over to reload and took a bullet right in the ear. His head snapped sideways. Blood and brain matter splattered toward me onto the floor. He'd been shot clean through the exterior wall of the cabin.

"My God," Ahmed said and tried to make himself as small as possible while hugging the floor. "Oh my God oh my God oh my God."

Everybody stopped firing. Mahmoud tensed up. He was getting ready to move. Ahmed looked beaten. Tariq was dead. He couldn't have felt or heard the round that instantly killed him.

No one was paying the slightest attention to me.

The cop with the bullhorn sounded seriously pissed off now.

"Come out with your hands up and no one else will get hurt!"

Ahmed and Mahmoud couldn't possibly shoot their way out of this. Surely they had to know that. But I wondered if any of the policemen were down.

I kept my body behind the wall of my room while peeking around the doorway. The bathtub would have been safer, but I had to know what was happening out there. Tariq had been shot. If Mahmoud and Ahmed were shot, I'd be free.

Mahmoud crept along the floor toward the front door.

"*Allahu Akbar*," he said. "*Allahu Akbar*." He kept saying it. And he stood when he reached the door.

"Come out with your hands up!"

Mahmoud wasn't going out with his hands up.

"*Allahu Akbar*," he said a final time before opening the door.

"No!" Ahmed said.

Mahmoud raised his shotgun toward the line of policemen as a storm of bullets tore his torso apart.

Horror washed over Ahmed's face as Mahmoud's pulverized body slumped onto the porch. He looked back at me with his mouth slack.

"Michael—" he said.

It was just him and me now.

He wanted me to say something, but I didn't know what to say.

"The rest of you come out with your hands up or *we will fire on you!*" the officer yelled, his voice much louder now that the door was wide open. Ahmed kicked it closed. He crawled toward Tariq's body, got blood all over himself, and took the gun from his friend's hand.

"Here," he said and slid it toward me. I gingerly took it. I knew it had a full magazine because I saw Tariq reload just before he was shot. "We'll make our last stand in your room," he said.

Oh no, we won't. If Ahmed came into in my room determined to martyr himself, the cops would blaze in and kill both of us.

"I'm not really much help to you," I said.

"You can shoot, right?" he said.

"Yeah," I said. "But I can hardly move."

"You don't need to move," he said. "Just sit up and shoot everyone who comes through the door."

He crept along the floor toward the window to get a last peek outside.

I knew what to do, but it was a lot harder than it had been in my fantasies.

Ahmed wasn't my friend. He was my kidnapper. He was responsible for the deaths of more than a dozen people that I knew of personally: two at the gas station and at least ten back at the bank. Mahmoud pulled the trigger, but it didn't matter. Ahmed was the leader. He'd surely spend the rest of his life in federal prison if the police could get their hands on him.

But he acted as though we had become friends. It seemed absurd to me, and I wondered if he really believed it, but he had just slid a fully loaded pistol to me across the floor.

Maybe he knew that I wasn't really converting to Islam, that I didn't really agree with his politics, that I was just playing along to buy time. Maybe he, too, was just playing along, pretending to believe because for him it was such a nice fantasy, like a lonely man pretending to feel loved by a prostitute. Like me pretending Ismail was a good person.

Ahmed only gave me one round to take into the bank. He knew I might shoot him and his friends. He knew. Perhaps he trusted me now, but maybe he figured it flat didn't matter anymore. He wasn't getting out of that cabin alive either way.

The truth did matter though. It mattered to me. It mattered to the police. And it mattered to Ahmed himself in his last moments.

As he peered over the lip of the shattered window for a last glance outside, I raised my pistol, swallowed hard, steadied my aim at his center of mass, and shot him. The pistol kicked in my grip. Ahmed convulsed as the bullet pierced the side of his rib cage, and he collapsed writhing onto the floor.

"Oh!" he said. "Michael! They shot me!"

He thrashed about and kicked the floor with the bottoms of his feet. I heard a radio squawk outside. "Shot fired inside," a policeman said.

"I think one of them shot himself, over," said another.

"Michael—" Ahmed said and reached his hand toward me.

He broke my heart.

"I shot you," I said.

"*You?*" he said. "But ... why?"

"You know why," I said and crawled toward him on the floor.

His face told me all I needed to know. He really had believed that I had gone over to him. And I felt at that moment like the most wicked person alive.

He clutched his side with his hand. Blood seeped between his fingers. His pistol lay on the floor next to him within reach. He glanced at it.

"Don't," I said and pointed my gun at him again.

He rolled onto his back and lay with his head on the floor, looking up at the ceiling. His arms went limp and he shook his head.

"Shoot me again," he said. "Put me out of my misery."

"Can't do that," I said. "It would be murder."

"Michael," he said and spit up blood. "You have already murdered me."

He turned his eyes toward me. They were tearing up slightly. I would have covered him with a blanket then if I had one.

I grabbed his pistol and slid it across the floor beyond his reach.

"Clear!" I yelled to the policemen outside. "Hostage coming out!"

"Come out with your hands up!" said the man with the bullhorn.

"I've been shot!" I called out. "I can only raise one arm!"

"Step out *slowly*!"

I struggled to stand, but I managed. I didn't even care about the pain anymore.

Ahmed looked up at me. He had his hands curled, fetuslike, in front of his chest. He was near death and his body knew it. His breathing was halting, labored. His eyes looked glassy and distant. His chest heaved. I'm not sure he recognized me anymore. I was hoping for a signal from him that he understood and forgave me, but even then I knew that in time I'd learn to get past it, that it was I who should forgive him and that I never would.

I stumbled onto the porch and squinted in the bright morning sunlight. More than two dozen men of the law pointed rifles at me.

"It's him," one of them said.

And they lowered their weapons.

Epilogue

I wish I could write that Ahmed survived, that I did not, in fact, murder him, and that he'll spend the rest of his life shackled in irons, but I can't. I'd have to make that ending up. Ahmed died of his wounds forty-one minutes after I shot him. Paramedics tried to keep him alive, and I'm even told they tried hard, but the bullet tore a hole in his lungs and he bled out internally.

I shouldn't say that I murdered him. Those were his words, not mine. He was less than sixty seconds away from sending both of us into the sky as Islamic martyrs. I had no other option. I tell myself that every day. Sometimes you just have to shoot people. Intellectually, I know it's true, but I don't always feel that it's true. I need a KA meeting. Killers Anonymous. Does such an organization exist? *My name is Michael. I shot a man who thought he was my friend, and I need some help.*

Mahmoud killed so many people. I can't understand it. Why didn't he feel the way I do about it? Pieces of that man were just missing. Maybe they're lying broken on the floor in a dungeon in Egypt. Maybe he wasn't born whole. I'll never know.

Ismail seemed to me like a whole person. Like a decent person, in fact. But he was a terrorist. He was part of a cell that ripped me from my home and my family. He was part of a cell that massacred innocent people like they were cattle on the killing floor of a slaughterhouse. I don't know if I'll ever resolve that contradiction.

I think about Ahmed every day. He's the only one of the four I think about every day. And I think I understood him before the end. He's right that the United States, simply by existing as a liberal secular superpower, poses an existential threat to his utopian fantasy. The entire modern world poses an existential threat to his utopian fantasy. He and his comrades chose to take up sword against that which threatens them. It is the way of the world. It always has been. And it always will be.

He wasn't born that way. Nor was he raised that way by his parents. He grew up in Seattle. He could have become a computer programmer, a literature professor, a bleeding-heart vegetarian, a Republican, a guitar player, a Navy SEAL, or a pothead. He and I might have been real friends had he done so, the kind of friends who don't shoot and kidnap each other.

For all the time he spent in this country, I don't think he ever truly understood it. Maybe it's just a conceit on my part, but I think I understood him better than he ever understood me. Had he known me the way my friends and family know me, he'd know I could never walk beside him on his dark road.

I haven't forgiven him for what he did to me and my family, but sometimes I pity him. Maybe that's a form of forgiveness. When he took me into that first house up in Washington, I wanted to pull him apart with my hands, but I've shuddered and cried more than once since I shot him. That's the most he'll ever get from me. He doesn't deserve even that much, but I think I need it.

The Idaho state police didn't charge me with murder. Nor did they charge me with bank robbery. I didn't think they would, but I nevertheless felt a hundred pounds lighter when they told me they wouldn't. Patty Hearst had to wait years for a pardon from the president of the United States, but the Idaho state police left me alone.

They let me call my wife Shelly on one of their phones. She didn't recognize the incoming-call number and had no idea it was me. "Hi, Sweetie," I told her. "It's me and I'm free." She broke down at once. We both did.

It's winter now. And though snow rarely falls on the valley floor where we live, the cold of early January seeps into everyone's bones. Sometimes it seems like sunlight never touches the street in front of my house. It certainly doesn't slant inside through the windows, not on the darkest days when the heavy dishrag sky strains to hold back an ocean of threatening rain over our heads. On those days, I feel like it is always miserable here and always will be, like sunshiny days are for other, luckier parts of the world.

But sometimes the sun comes out even in January, and when it does, I like to get in my car and drive up to the lower slopes of Mount Hood, just an hour to the east, where three times as much rain falls as it does in the city, and spend hours on trails beneath dripping evergreens, the pyramid spire of the great mountain looming in the sky like a planet of ice that's almost, but not quite, within reach. The rainforests on the western slope of that mountain—with their mosses, their year-round riot of ferns, and their verdant Christmas-tree smell—are places where politics and religion from the other side of the world have no purchase.

Shelly and I are planning to move soon. We'll buy a new house through a secret third party and we'll have a separate mailing address. Not even a private detective will be able to find us, at least not very easily.

In the meantime, we sleep with our bedroom door bolted from the inside and with bars on the windows. They don't help much. I don't sleep well. The bed feels slanted. It's not—I checked using a construction level I keep in the basement—but sometimes I feel like I'm going to slide off and fall. When the heated mattress is on and I'm lying with my wife with our cats at our feet, I can lull myself into a state of relative comfort. But sleep itself comes with a price. Someday I may dream sweetly again. I'll be happy to not dream at all.

I don't always dream of captivity, though. Sometimes I dream of people whose faces I can't quite make out in the middle of a great sandy desert. They've fashioned an idyllic village from stone for themselves atop a series of underground springs where palm trees provide food for the winter and shade during summer. They live settled lives. Little has changed over the centuries. They're pious people. Muslims. And they're peaceful. The place where they live would charm any tourist who found it.

But masked men emerge on horseback from the deeper parts of

the desert, places so hot and arid and hostile that not even Bedouin nomads on camelback go. They come at night with swords raised high, their thunderous steeds pounding sand with their hooves, riding under a black flag in the moonlight.

Turn the page for a special preview of

Michael J. Totten's

Where the West Ends

What you just finished reading was fiction.
What you're about to read isn't.

.

Back to Iraq

An adventure," the great travel writer Tim Cahill once wrote, "is never an adventure when it happens. An adventure is simply physical and emotional discomfort recollected in tranquility." I have never taken a trip that more aptly fits that description than when my best friend Sean LaFreniere and I drove to Iraq on a whim.

It was stupid of us and the trip was unrelentingly miserable, though in my defense the idea was not solely mine. Sean was my accomplice and we suffered together.

I lived in Beirut at the time. He lived in Copenhagen, where he was studying for his Master's in architecture. I invited him to Beirut, but he said he would rather see Turkey, so instead we met in Istanbul. Neither of us had any idea that we would end up driving all the way to Iraq. Why would we? Hardly any tourists visiting Turkey even think of it. Istanbul is one of the world's greatest cities while Iraq is—well, it's Iraq.

Sean's plane was a day late due to an airline snafu, and he arrived exhausted and grumpy. "I need a drink," he said. "Is it even possible to get a drink in this country?"

"This is Turkey!" I said. "You can get a drink in even the smallest mountain village in Anatolia." He knew that already, but he was tired and had forgotten. I had been to only one Muslim country that bans alcohol, and that was Libya. It's available most other places.

"Come on, Sean," I said. "Let's get you a drink."

We washed down bloody steaks with smoky red wine in a brick and stone building that was older than our own country while a man in a tuxedo masterfully played the violin. I dearly wished I could have been there with my wife. The restaurant's atmosphere was achingly romantic and I hadn't seen her for months. Sean missed his wife, too. Angie, like my wife Shelly, was back in the United States.

But Sean and I had a man's trip ahead of us. He and I both love hitting the open road in a car, especially in foreign countries. It is not our wives' style. When he and I are in the mood for a road trip, we go alone.

I let Sean decide the itinerary since I'd been to Turkey before and he hadn't. The city of Izmir on the Aegean coast is spectacular, but we only had three days before he had to return for exams and I had to catch a flight to Tel Aviv. So the plan was to visit Gallipoli and Troy which were much closer.

We hurtled down the highway from Istanbul toward Gallipoli. That road heads west in the direction of Greece and Sicily. On the way we argued about whether Turkey was Eastern or Western. In the twenty-four hours since he had arrived, he decided it was mostly Western. I played Devil's Advocate and said it was Eastern, though what I really think is that it's neither and both.

Many visitors to Istanbul are surprised that, aside from the mosques on the skyline, it looks much more European than Middle Eastern. They shouldn't be. Although part of the city is on the Asian side of the Bosphorus strait, most of it is in Europe. It was the eastern capital of the Roman Empire and endured as such for centuries after the western half, with Rome as its capital, first declined and then fell. It was not until 1453 that the city, then named Constantinople and the capital of the Byzantine Empire, was conquered by Turkish Ottomans out of Asia. The Ottoman Empire then ruled over most of the Middle East and much of Europe's Balkan Peninsula for hundreds of years. The empire was Islamic and ruled by a caliphate, but it was also, simultaneously, trans-civilizational.

Many Europeans in Bosnia and Albania converted to Islam during this time, but the Turks couldn't resist becoming a little Westernized by incorporating Europeans into their realm. Turkey is thoroughly Western compared with its cousin Turkmenistan, which isn't at all. The same phenomenon partly explains why Russia today has Eastern aspects to its culture due to its conquering of lands in the Far East and why Mexico and Peru are culturally part Aztec and Incan despite being the former colonies of Western imperial Spain.

"Be careful out there!" Sean's Danish friends said, as though Turkey were teeming with Islamist fanatics who wanted to kill him. "Isn't it dangerous?" one of his professors said. "Don't let anyone know you're American or living in Denmark!" Little did this educated man know, Istanbul is safer than Copenhagen.

Danes were right to be a little concerned, though. The Danish newspaper *Jyllands-Posten* had recently published a batch of cartoons of the Prophet Muhammad that Muslims all over the world considered "blasphemous." Frenzied mobs sponsored by the Syrian government set Denmark's embassies in Beirut and Damascus on fire. One hundred and thirty nine people, almost all of them Muslims, were killed during various protests worldwide.

Istanbul looked and felt more Western than Sean expected. It felt Western to me, too, since I had just arrived from the Arab world. I was still in Devil's Advocate mode, though, so it was my job to make the case for Turkey being Eastern.

"Remember," I said. "This country borders Greece and Bulgaria. But it also borders Iraq."

I could all but hear the gears turn in his head.

"That's right," he said and put his hand over his mouth. He knew he shouldn't say what he was thinking, but he removed his hand and said it anyway. "Holy shit, we could drive to Iraq."

The instant he said it I knew that we would, indeed, drive to Iraq. Who cares about Troy when we could drive to *Iraq*?

I have known Sean most of my life. I should have known, then, that it's impossible for us to rent a car in a foreign country and only drive a few hours, that he and I would almost certainly end up more than a thousand miles and a whole world away from where we innocently planned to visit over the weekend. He is the only person I grew up with in Oregon, with the possible exception of my brother, Scott, who would see any appeal whatsoever in driving from a pleasant and heavily-touristed part of the world to one of the scariest countries on earth.

But Sean didn't yet know what I knew. I had just flown over Turkey's Anatolian core in an airplane on a clear day from Lebanon. All of Turkey east of the Bosphorus ripples with mountains. And when I say mountains, I mean *mountains*. Huge, steep, snow-covered monsters that rise from the earth and the sea like impassable walls. Turkey is a miniature continent unto itself. (Hence the name Asia Minor.) You can't blow through that land in a car like you can if you stick to I-5 in California.

I wanted to do it, though. Badly. How many people have ever decided to spontaneously take a road trip to Iraq from Europe after they were already in the car and driving in the other direction? We were heading toward Greece, not the Tigris. We had no visas. No map. No plan. And no time. Sean had to be back in Copenhagen in three days for his exams. Pulling this off would be nearly impossible. Nothing appealed to me more.

I pulled off the road and stopped the car so I could think.

"We're going to make this work," I said.

Why go to Iraq? Because it is there, because it is different, and because no one else wants to. Because adventurous travel and unusual human experiences make our lives better. Istanbul is spectacular and Paris is even more so, but visiting a place like Iraq engages the senses and the mind on a much deeper level even if it is unpleasant. It's not like going to another planet, exactly, but it's new enough and *strange* enough that it makes me feel like a kid again when everything was hard and had to be learned. Iraq is so different from my native Oregon that almost everything about it is utterly fascinating. Istanbul is Eastern enough and exotic enough for it to be interesting for a short while, but at the same time it's enough like the West I grew up in that it begins to feel mundanely familiar within a few days, if not hours. A sudden arrival in an utterly alien culture is as intoxicating as a narcotic.

I called my wife and told her what I was up to. I also called a friend of mine who worked for the Council of Ministers in Erbil, the capital of Iraq's autonomous Kurdish region just across the Turkish border. I had visited Iraqi Kurdistan just three months earlier as a journalist, so I knew some people. And I needed to know: would it be possible to get tourist visas on arrival at the border?

"Michael!" my Iraqi friend said, disappointed that I even asked. "You know the Kurds won't give you any problems."

Iraqi Kurds, unlike Iraqi Arabs, are some of the most pro-American people in the world.

"Sorry," I said. "The border is more than a thousand miles away. I don't want to drive all the way over there in winter unless I'm sure we can get in."

"Of course you can get in," he said. "You are always welcome in Kurdistan."

"Can I call you from the border if we have any problems?" I said.

"Michael!" he said. "We will not give you any trouble. The only people who might give you trouble are Turks."

I didn't think the Turks would care if or how we left Turkey. They might care once we tried to come back, but Sean and I had multiple-entry visas.

It soon dawned on Sean that we were actually going to Iraq. (Even though we would be in the tranquil and friendly Kurdistan region as opposed to war-torn Fallujah.) We were no longer talking about it, but doing it.

"Would you take your wife there?" he said.

"Of course," I said. "It's really not dangerous. Shelly wished she could have gone with me when I went there before."

Iraqi Kurds have never been at war with the United States. Nearly every man, woman, and child was relieved when Saddam Hussein's regime was demolished. Their part of the country suffered no insurgency, no kidnappings, almost no crime, and even less terrorism.

It was a minor drag that Sean and I wouldn't get to see much of Turkey except from the car. Gallipoli isn't the most interesting place in the country, but it was the site of a crucial World War I battle and the inspiration for one of the most moving speeches of Mustafa Kemal Ataturk, modern Turkey's founder.

"Those heroes that shed their blood and lost their lives," he famously said of the buried British dead, "you are now lying in the soil of a friendly country. Therefore rest in peace. There is no difference between the Johnnies and the Mehmets to us, where they lie, side by side here in this country of ours. You, the mothers who sent their sons from faraway countries, wipe away your tears. Your sons are now lying in our bosom and are in peace. After having lost their lives on this land, they have become our sons as well."

The only things we didn't have that we needed were a decent map and a good night's sleep.

We crossed the surging Dardanelles by rain-spattered ferry and landed on Turkey's Asian shore in the charming town of Canakkale.

Gallipoli was just on the other side of the water. A monumental set piece downtown was made of big guns from the battle.

I asked the clerk at the hotel desk if he knew where I could buy a map.

He didn't. I wasn't surprised. Maps are generally harder to find in the Near and Middle East where a startling number of people don't know how to read them.

"Do you have any idea what's the best road to take to get to Turkish Kurdistan?" I said. Sean and I did have a map; it just wasn't a good one. We couldn't tell from the low granularity which route was best.

He didn't answer the question. Instead he said, "I don't like Kurds."

"What's wrong with Kurds?" Sean said.

"I don't like their culture," the clerk said and twisted his face. "They're dirty and stupid."

Sean and I just looked at him and blinked. He seemed like such a sweet kid when he checked us in.

I had a brief flashback to a conversation I had with a Kurd in Northern Iraq a few weeks earlier. "Istanbul is a great city," my Kurdish friend said. "The only problem is it's full of *Turks*."

"What do you think of Arabs?" Sean said.

"Eh," the clerk said. "We don't like them in Turkey. We have the same religion, but that's it. They cause so many problems. You know."

Sometimes it seems like everyone in the Middle East hates everyone else in the Middle East. Arabs hate Kurds and Israelis. Turks hate Arabs and Kurds. Kurds hate Turks and fear Arabs. (Intriguingly, Kurds love Israelis.) Everyone hates Palestinians.

Not all people are haters. I know plenty who aren't. But every culture has its baseline prejudices that individuals either opt into or out of. It's exhausting. Sometimes I just want to shake people and say: *Keep your old-world ethnic squabbling out of my face, willya please? Jesus, no wonder there's so much war around here.* Even so, Middle Easterners are the most friendly and charming people I've ever met.

Sean and I tried to go to sleep early so we could leave at first light. I stared at the ceiling and remembered my flight over the spectacularly mountainous country. *We're screwed*, I thought. *There's no way we can drive across that landscape to Iraq and back in three days from where we are now.*

And I was right.

Sean and I woke at dawn and headed south from Canakkale toward the ancient ruins of Troy. We wouldn't have time to hang out there, though, or anywhere else for that matter, if we wanted to make it all the way to Iraq and back to Istanbul on time.

We weren't in the car for a half-hour before we saw the turnoff.

"We have to stop," Sean said.

"No time," I said.

"It's Troy!" Sean said. "We can't just drive past it."

I pulled off the road. Vicious dogs ran straight at the car. If I hadn't slammed on the brakes I would have killed them. This happened over and over again while driving through Turkey.

We parked in the lot and paid twenty or so dollars to get in.

"Hurry," I said to Sean. "Grab your camera and go."

Somebody built a wooden yet somehow cartoon-looking "Trojan Horse" and stuck it directly outside what would have been the gate to the city had it not been reduced to rubble by time, neglect, and erosion. Sean ran toward it while I snapped a quick picture.

"Run," he said.

We ran—literally, ran—through the entire ruined city in under ten minutes. It's amazing how small the place is. This tiny little town, no bigger than a dinky modern-day village, left an imprint on history and literature completely out of proportion to its actual size. Too bad we had no time whatsoever to contemplate any of it.

We ran back to the car. I damn near killed the dogs again on the way back to the main road. Do they snarl and charge at everyone who drives past? It's a wonder they're still alive.

I unfurled a brand-new map we picked up from a tourist information office. It looked like the best bet was to drive down to the Aegean Coast toward Izmir, a city we initially deemed too far away from Istanbul to visit in time. We couldn't possibly get all the way to Iraq and back in the two days we had left, but we kept going anyway. If by some miracle we could figure out how to get there on schedule, we'd have no time to do anything but have lunch and leave. We were driving 2,000 miles round-trip—to Iraq of all places—just to have lunch.

I drove us toward Izmir as fast as the coastal road would allow. The Aegean Sea sprawled out on the right. The view was extraordinary. Greece was on the other side of that water. I could see it. There were more islands between us and the Greek mainland than I could count on two hands. While beautiful, the view was also discouraging. Greece is a long way from Iraq. It's more than a thousand road miles away. And yet there it was.

The way south toward Izmir was a nightmare of slow-moving traffic around tight bends in the road and through coastal resorts. Izmir was at most five percent of the way to Iraq from Istanbul. We had driven almost half a day and still hadn't made it even that far. There was no way we could make it to Iraq in even a week at that speed.

"We need to head inland and get off this road," I said.

"The mountains will kill us," Sean said.

"The coast is killing us. We have to chance it."

I turned off and headed toward the heart of Anatolia. At first the road was encouraging. Then we got stuck behind truckers doing 20 miles an hour.

"Told you this was a bad idea," Sean said.

"The coast was a bad idea, too," I said. "We're pretty much screwed no matter what."

We pressed on into hard driving rain, which slowed us down even more. I wanted to blow up the slow trucks ahead with a rocket launcher. *Get out of the way, get out of the way, we're making terrible time!* Eventually the rain cleared, revealing a punishing road toward a gigantic mountainous wall.

"Oh my *God*!" Sean said. "We never should have turned inland."

He was right. I screwed up, but it was too late.

"We'll head back to the coast when we can," I said.

We didn't make it back to the coast until dark. This time we were on the Mediterranean. Rain washed over the road in broad sheets. In a third of our available time, almost no progress had been made at all toward Iraq.

We both woke up with a virus. My throat burned when I swallowed. My entire body, from the top of my head to the bottoms of my feet, was wracked with a terrible fever ache. We had so far to go and almost no time to do it. At least we were out of the punishing mountains.

But we were back on the punishing coast. A twisty little road hugged the shore which rose up so sheer from the Mediterranean it was impossible to drive more than 30 miles an hour without plunging shriekingly over a cliff.

"Now you see why I wanted to get off the coast!" I said.

Sean nodded silently. There was no way to win. You just can't drive across Turkey in a normal amount of time unless you take the autobahn linking Istanbul and Ankara. We were so far from that road, though, that it was very near hopeless.

I tried to sleep in the passenger seat while Sean took the wheel. There would be no more stopping to sleep in hotels. We would have to drive straight for the rest of the trip.

Without time to stop at restaurants, we were forced to eat terrible food. We had soft drinks, potato chips, and other crap from convenience stores attached to gas stations that carried the same kind of salty, sugary snacks sold in similar stores in the United States.

Once we tried to pop into a little food stall at night. Then we saw what was being cooked on a stove: a nasty green-brown substance bubbling in an unspeakable cauldron. We both turned and walked right out the door.

"I can't deal with that right now," I said.

"It looks like Orc food," Sean said.

In troglodyte country, where some people live in caves tunneled into the ground and the cliffs, an old man stood by the side of the road selling bananas.

"Want some bananas?" I said.

"Yes!" Sean said.

I pulled off the road.

"Quick, get those bananas," I said.

Sean rolled down the window and handed the old man a dollar. In return we received a handful of bananas. Real food at last.

We passed through great-looking towns that I cannot tell you the names of. Turkey is packed with wonderful places that hardly anyone in the States ever hears about.

The virus was killing me.

"We need a pharmacy," I said.

"No time to stop," Sean said.

"If we're going to drive all day and all night we can't be feeling like this," I said. "We'll drive off the road and kill both of us."

We stopped at a pharmacy and bought medicine.

We also stopped at an Internet café. Sean and I wouldn't be able to take our rental car across the border into Iraq. If we wanted to make our way to the Iraqi city of Duhok, someone would have to pick us up. So I sent an email to one of my fixers and tried to hire him for the next day. I asked him to please send someone else to meet us if he couldn't do it himself.

Sean and I got back in the car. A few hours later we could stop at another Internet café, check the email again, and continue to work on our Iraqi logistics. We didn't yet know that there would be no more Internet cafés. We'd be flying blind from then on.

I felt amazingly irresponsible for trying to put together an Iraqi itinerary at the last second from the road while sick and with no time.

"If no one picks us up," I said to Sean, "we'll have to hitchhike or flag down a taxi."

"Hitchhike in Iraq?" Sean said.

"Sure," I said. "It's the Kurds in Northern Iraq. They're cool."

Sean didn't say anything. I knew how dubious what I suggested must have sounded.

"Are you okay with that?" I said. "Will you cross the border if no one is there to pick us up? We'll figure something out. Trust me. Trust the Kurds. Trust the universe. We'll be fine."

"Alright," Sean said and threw his hands in the air.

We continued the punishing drive along the coast, in the rain, malnourished, sleep-deprived, and wracked with a terrible illness. It was unspeakable.

"Holy shit, look at that!" Sean said as we drove past some hotels on the side of the road.

"What?" I said.

"A sea castle," Sean said. "Wait, you'll see it again in a second."

I saw it when we cleared the bank of hotels.

"Holy shit!" I said and pulled off to the side of the road.

An otherworldly sea castle appeared to literally float off the coast of the Mediterranean. I had never even heard of this thing.

"Wow," Sean said. "Look what they have! This country is just amazing."

"Yep," I said. "We need to come back here and visit it properly."

"Let's go, let's go," he said. "It's getting dark."

It was, indeed, getting dark. The cold medicine we bought at the pharmacy seemed to have no effect. We were both sick as dogs and had no time to stop at a hotel to sleep it off.

BANG. We got a flat tire. I pulled onto the shoulder.

"So much for Iraq," Sean said.

"Wait," I said. "We might have a spare."

I popped the trunk. We did have a spare! It was a real spare, too, not a near-useless "donut" that can fall off at speeds faster than thirty miles an hour. The only problem was we had no jack.

Sean and I walked across the road and ducked into a store that sold yard tools. The owner did not speak a word of English. Darkness was falling. Sean drew a picture of a blown out tire on a pad of paper. The man indicated he didn't sell tires. I grabbed the pad of paper and drew a picture of a car propped up on a jack.

The man called a friend of his who showed up on a motorcycle with a big bag of tools. Without saying a word or even looking at us he jacked up our car and changed the tire for us in two minutes. I handed our savior twenty dollars.

"Thank you so much!" I said. He rode away on his bike.

And then we were off. The whole flat tire incident only took half an hour. What incredible luck. We just might make it to Iraq after all.

We drove all night, taking turns at the wheel in the dark. I could tell when we finally left the Mediterranean and approached inland Turkish Kurdistan after the silhouettes of palm trees vanished and I could see semi-desert features at the edge of the headlight range. Most traffic slacked off by this point. Towns grew poorer and farther apart. Syria was only a few miles off to our right. Turkey didn't look remotely like Europe any more. That much was obvious even in the dark. We were deep in the Middle East now.

"I can't drive anymore," Sean said. "You have to do it."

I got behind the wheel and drove as far as I could until three o'clock in the morning.

"You have to drive now," I said. "I'm going to go off the road if I drive any farther."

"I can't drive anymore," Sean said.

I stopped the car and got out. My teeth instantly chattered. It was absolutely frigid outside. If we napped on the side of the road we would shake inside our coats. My entire body still throbbed with fever ache. I needed a bed.

"We can't sleep now," I said as I got back in the car. "You have no idea how cold it is here. We need to find a hotel."

But we were in the absolute middle of nowhere. All I could see were rocks and scrub in the headlights.

I drove slowly so I would not kill us. We found a low-rent Turkish trucker motel. What looked like 900 trucks were outside.

"I'm stopping here," I said.

"I don't want to spend the night with a bunch of loud truckers," Sean said. The parking lot was awfully noisy.

"There's nothing else out here," I said. "It's either the truckers, the cold, or I kill us on the side of the road."

We went into the trucker motel in the middle of the Turkish wasteland on the road to Iraq. It was exactly as grim inside as you would expect. A twitchy man on the night shift checked us into a room.

"Sozpas," I said. *Thank you,* in Kurdish.

"Are you sure you're speaking the right language?" Sean said. "Are we really in Kurdistan?"

"I don't know," I said. "I think so, but I'm not sure. Anyway, he did not seem offended." He probably was, however, surprised. The Turkish government had only recently begun to relent in its draconian suppression of the Kurdish language.

It was four o'clock in the morning. We set our alarm clocks for six. Two hours later we woke. I felt exhausted and needed to sleep for a week. My eyes burned from the light. But I felt great at the same time. My fever had broken. And it was time to head into Iraq.

Sean and I dragged our sorry, exhausted, malnourished selves to the car at 6:30 in the morning just a few hours northwest of the Turkish-Iraqi border. For the first time we had a look at our new surroundings in daylight.

Turkish Kurdistan is a disaster. It is emphatically not where you want to go on vacation.

One village after another had been blown to pieces by tank shells and air strikes. Military bunkers, loaded with sand bags and bristling with mounted machine guns, were set up all over the place. Helicopters flew overhead. An army foot patrol marched toward us alongside the highway. Twenty-four soldiers brandished rifles across their chests. I slowed the car down as we approached so I would not make them nervous. I could see the whites of their eyes as they stared, deadly serious, at me through the windshield. Neither of us dared take their pictures. Those soldiers were not just hanging out and they were not messing around.

The civil war in Eastern Turkey didn't look anything like it was over. I could tell just from driving through that the Marxist-Leninist Kurdistan Workers' Party (the PKK) was still active. How else to explain the full-on siege by the army? The Turks' treatment of Kurds has been horrific since the founding of the republic, but the separatist

PKK seems hell-bent on matching the Turks with the worst it can muster, including the deliberate murder of Kurdish as well as Turkish and foreign civilians.

The highway ran right alongside the Syrian border for a stretch. Turkey had walled off the deranged Baathist regime of Hafez and Bashar al-Assad with a mile-wide swath of land mines wrapped in barbed wire and marked with skulls and crossbones. At one point we could look right into a Syrian town in the distance where Kurds lived in possibly worse conditions than even in Turkey. While many, if not most, Turkish nationalists have a near-ideological hatred of Kurdish nationalism, the Arab nationalist regime in Damascus is worse. At least the Turkish government is elected and the Kurds get to vote. The Assad regime is a totalitarian monster that stripped many Syrian Kurds of their citizenship solely for the "crime" of not being Arab.

From a distance it appears that the biggest problem in the Middle East is radical Islam. Islamism surely is the worst of the Middle East's exported problems, but up close the biggest source of conflict seems to be ethnic nationalism and sectarianism, at least in the Eastern Mediterranean where no state is homogenous. The crackup of the Ottoman Empire has yet to settle down into anything stable. Arab nationalism, Turkish nationalism, and Kurdish nationalism everywhere create bloody borders and internal repression. And that's just for starters. Lebanese went at other Lebanese for fifteen long years. Sunni and Shia death squads mercilessly "cleansed" whole swaths of Iraq of the other. Syria's Alawite minority was using the state to violently suppress the Sunni majority.

Every Kurdish village I saw still standing in Eastern Turkey looked grim and forlorn compared with those I had seen in Iraq. The only places in Turkish Kurdistan that looked pleasant, from the main road at least, were those where no people lived, where the army hadn't dug in, where there was no visible poverty, where there were no blown up buildings, and where you did not look across minefields toward Syria.

Sean and I soon came upon the city of Cizre that straddled the

Tigris River on its winding way to Iraq. I was glad we didn't spend the night there. It didn't look like a war zone, as parts of the countryside did, but it did look sketchy and miserable. Most businesses were shuttered behind filthy metal garage-style doors. Apartment buildings that looked like low-rise versions of communist public housing units in the former Soviet Union sulked behind crumbling walls. Utterly gone was the quasi-Victorian architecture of central Istanbul, the lovely classical Ottoman-era homes of the mountain interior, and the typically Mediterranean look and feel of the southern coast.

Sean documented the misery with his camera while I drove until I saw, just up ahead, a flatbed truck loaded with armed men who looked like guerrillas.

"Quick, put down the camera," I said. "Don't take a picture of *those* guys."

They wore keffiyehs on their heads. Only Arabs and Kurds wear keffiyehs. Turks never do, at least none that I've seen. These guys were heavily armed and sloppily dressed. They obviously were not Turkish military. They may have been PKK fighters or they may have been what the Kurds call *Jash*.

The Jash, or donkeys, are "very well paid Kurdish mercenaries that the Turkish government use against the PKK," said a man I know in Iraq's Kurdistan Regional Government. "Many Turkish soldiers aren't well trained (in most cases don't have the courage) to fight a guerrilla war in the uncontrollable Kurdish mountains. To save the lives of their soldiers, the Turks hired some local Kurds and paid them very well to fight the PKK on their behalf. During the 1980s Saddam's regime did the same. He hired locals, mostly escapees from military service, and gave them money and arms. But after the 1991 uprising all of the Iraqi Kurdish *Jash* failed Saddam and helped the [Kurdish fighters] as they liberated the Iraqi Kurdistan towns and cities one after one."

As I slowly drove onto a bridge over the Tigris, I noticed that every driver in oncoming traffic stared at us nervously. The vibe on the streets was palpably paranoid even from inside the car. It's so easy to misunderstand what's going on in a strange foreign land, especially when you don't walk around and talk to people, but it was clear that the situation in Cizre in early 2006 was not good.

No one is allowed to drive a passenger car from Turkey into Iraq. Only trucks are allowed to cross over. And the truck inspection line stretched for miles.

So Sean and I left the rental car and our non-essential luggage in a gravel lot near the customs gate. We stuffed everything we needed—passports, cash, phone numbers, etc.—into our backpacks and started walking. I sure hoped my Kurdish fixer sent somebody to pick us up. We had long been out of email contact, however, and there was no way to know until we got to the other side.

As we approached the first building we were instantly mobbed by a crowd of gritty middle-aged men.

"Taxi."

"Taxi."

"You need a taxi."

"We're walking across," Sean said.

"You can't walk across," a man said. "Give me your passports." He stuck out his hand. "Come on, give me your passports."

"Who are you?" I said in my *don't-fuck-with-me* voice as I sized him up head to toe. He smelled distinctly like trouble.

"I'm a police officer," he said.

Liar, I thought. Did he think we were stupid? He wore shabby clothes, not an officer's uniform. And he had the obvious personality of a shake-down artist or braying carpet shop tout.

"Come with me," he said.

I trusted that he knew the border procedure, but I would not hand him my passport. He led Sean and me into a small room in a trailer where a real police officer sat behind a desk. The officer asked for our passports. We handed them over, he wrote down our names, then handed our passports back.

"Here," our 'guide' said. "Get in this taxi." He opened the back door of a yellow taxi.

"Why?" I said.

"Just get in," Sean said, annoyed with my resistant attitude. He got in the back. I climbed in after him. Two strangers, both of them men, hopped in with us. One had horrible pink scars all over his face and his hands.

"Why do we need a taxi?" I said. "I'd rather walk."

"No one can walk across this border, my friend," our fake policeman-driver-guide said. "It will cost fifty dollars."

"*Fifty dollars?*" I said. "For what? For a one-minute drive down the street? Come on."

Sean put his hand on my shoulder. He was feeling much more patient than I. I was sleep-deprived and cranky, and I had been shaken down in Egypt and Jordan recently and was in no mood for more.

"Did you notice what happened back there?" Sean said to me quietly. "We jumped to the front of the line and no one complained."

He was right. There *was* a huge line of people waiting for taxis. Mr. Fake Police Officer Man yanked us right to the front. I decided to cut him some slack. Yes, he was ripping us off. But he was also speeding things up.

We pulled up to the side of a building. The man with the horrible pink scars on his face got out.

"Follow that man," our driver said. "He knows what to do."

We followed him to a drive-thru type window and handed our passports to the border official. He stamped us out of the country and we were set.

"Do you know why that man's face looks like that?" Sean said on our way back to the taxi.

"No," I said. "Do you?"

"He's Iraqi," Sean said. "Those scars are burns from chemical weapons. I've seen photos online. I know that's what happened to him."

We drove through a wasteland of devastated buildings, piles of scrap metal and box cars, an unfinished international highway, and derelict drive-thru gates that presumably were closed after the deranged behavior of Saddam's regime required a shutdown of the Turkish side of the border. After a quick hop over a one-way bridge we were inside Iraq. The Iraqi side was cleaner, more orderly, more prosperous, and far softer on the eyes than the Turkish side. I swear it felt like the sun came out and the birds started chirping as we left Eastern Turkey behind.

An Iraqi Kurdish guard stood in front of the customs house wearing a crisp professional uniform.

"Choni!" I said. *Hello*, in Kurdish.

Everyone in the car flashed him our passports. He smiled and waved us past a sign that said "Welcome to Iraqi Kurdistan Region."

Inside the immigration office a bad Syrian soap opera played on TV. We were told to sit down in the waiting area after turning in our passports at the front desk. A young man brought us overflowing glasses of hot sticky brown tea on little plates with dainty spoons.

"Well," Sean said as he nervously flicked his eyes around the room. "We're here."

You can purchase a trade paperback copy of Where the West Ends *from Amazon.com, Barnes & Noble, Powell's Books, and other fine bookstores. Electronic editions are also available.*

Made in the USA
Charleston, SC
19 March 2013